Carnival

By the Same Author

Carnival

Harold Rhenisch

The Porcupine's Quill

CANADIAN CATALOGUING IN PUBLICATION DATA

Rhenisch, Harold, 1958–
Carnival

ISBN 0-88984-213-2

I. Title.

PS8585.H54C37 2000   C813'.54   C00-930398-7
PR9199.3.R43C37 2000

Published by The Porcupine's Quill,
68 Main Street, Erin, Ontario NOB 1TO.
Readied for the press by John Metcalf; copy edited by Doris Cowan.
Typeset in Trump, printed on Zephyr Antique laid,
and bound at The Porcupine's Quill Inc.

Sections of this manuscript have appeared elsewhere:
'Martha' in the Queen's Quarterly and 'The Rape' in Quarry.

Represented in Canada by the Literary Press Group.
Trade orders are available from General Distribution Services.

We acknowledge the support of the Ontario Arts Council,
and the Canada Council for the Arts for our publishing program.
The financial support of the Government of Canada
through the Book Publishing Industry Development Program
is also gratefully acknowledged.

I 2 3 4 • 02 01 00

Canada

for Hans Rhenisch

Every visitor to the orchard that was my childhood home heard the
stories of a boy and his best friend coming of age in Kuppenheim, a
small town across the Rhine from Strasbourg, during the Second
World War. As boys, my brother and I must have heard those stories a hundred times. Life on that farm, and the manner in which
my father's German past gave us the mixed country of Canada and
Germany which was the British Columbia of our childhood, I have
already described in my book *Out of the Interior: The Lost Country*. As the farming became ever more compromised and alcohol
became increasingly the means of setting aside the stress of the
loss of cherished dreams, the stories became ever more fantastical.
The Germany they described, a world of castles, wild boars, and
escaped French POWS, as well as the life of heroism and total disre-
gard for authority they set within it, took on a great importance for
us. My brother and I made sure that we were present whenever the
stories were told, for at each telling they were more heroic, magi-
cal, and mythical than the time before – my father was justly
renowned as one of the great story-tellers of the Okanagan Valley.
Then came the abandonment of alcohol. The stories shrank
overnight to simple narratives of concrete facts, narrated like
newspaper reports. In the process, they gained considerable emo-
tional strength, but they also lost their ability to describe a world –
which just happened to be the country of my childhood. I was sad-
dened by its loss.

In 1984, I recorded my father telling his stories, in a last hope of
capturing their quality of continual transmutation. After we had
filled eight hours of tape, my father sat back in his chair, tears running down his face, his voice cracked, and said, 'Good. I don't have
to remember all that any more.' He has never told the stories since.
During those eight hours, however, he gave me stories he had
never shared before, including the terrible stories of the gang rape
and bloody death of his childhood sweetheart, Maria, the horrific
retribution for her death, and the story of his abject fear while
being hunted by an American in a fighter plane, just for sport.
These stories and the dissociation they introduced into my father's
life centre this book. In writing them down, I found I was not a

detached observer, and over the following years my identity as a Canadian was completely transformed. I learned German, made three trips to Germany to understand the roots of my connection with that distant country, and collected more stories from my father's brothers and sisters. Surprisingly, they corroborated my father's stories completely. One of my cousins had even received many of the same stories from his father, my uncle Michael, and had spent his childhood living within them, just as I had done. Our journey is the same.

For the last eleven years I have lived with these stories as my own. I have succeeded at bringing the magic back to them, but it is not my father's lost magic – I found that irretrievable. To my astonishment, the magic in these stories is the magic I received from them as a boy in a Similkameen farmhouse kitchen thirty years ago. I had never even suspected the existence of that world or its importance, but it is fitting that in the end it has come alive.

My father and I, who have quite differing personalities, occasionally share one in this book, as I help him understand the more difficult parts of his story and he brings me the more hidden roots of my own, but the stories themselves are exactly as they happened, and many passages, some long, some short, are in my father's own words. This is, however, above all a work of fiction, and its story, of the forces unleashed in 1930s Germany and of their terrible retribution, of an entire generation raised without parents or history, confronting the worst horrors of our species without the insulation or protection of society, the consequent death of civilization and of the world of story – and its eventual and unexpected re-creation – is a story, as my father well knew, that has needed to be told for fifty-three years.

Harold Rhenisch,
26 January 1987, Keremeos
6 July 1998, 108 Mile Ranch

I know thy works, that thou art neither cold nor hot:
I would thou wert cold or hot.

Revelation 3: 15

1. The Town

A Town Flying over the Forest on Silver Wings

In the town where I was born, storks nest on sooty chimneypots above red brick roofs. The skies are grey, heavy with rain. The streets are black, knotted. The houses have deep roots, thrusting up cobbles unevenly so you stumble and sink and sometimes almost swim down the street. Even in the haze of summer, when the light piles up in the air, it is a grey world. Storks look down from the steep, scattered roofs into gardens of cabbages, walled in with sticks dragged down from the forest and broken piles of bricks from the city wall, where our people – when God walked among them with his wooden helmet, nettle juice smeared on his cheeks and his rawhide shield trimmed with eelskin – held out against the Swedes two hundred years ago.

On Sundays the bells call out, back and forth from village to village, rippling the grain in the lower fields and splintering in the trees on the hills behind us. Our bell rings over them all, shouting against the roofs and breaking over them like a wave on a rough shore, but breaking in their shape, until our whole town is a picture of sound, growing larger everywhere you look, as the bell tolls and swells over all the other bells from all the other towns around.

The First Story That Children Learn

The Swedes burned the forests, rode down the wild boars, and trampled the fields into mud. They surrounded our town, trying to flush out Wallenstein, who had raided their armies up and down the Rhine. When winter came, when our people had nearly starved and the children lay quietly in their beds, too weak to move – when there were no more chickens flapping through the rafters, angels flying and rustling as you went to sleep – the Swedes thought our town would die; they thought they had Wallenstein at last, but instead of raising a white flag and opening the gate, Wallenstein loaded the cannon with the last hard, black loaves of bread and fired them through the rain. The bread was all our people had left, but the Swedes were running short of food, too – after all, they had stripped and ruined the whole area! When the bread landed in their camp, they packed up and left in disgust.

Ja, so Mama told me when I was a boy, as the wind blew at the white curtains, and the smell of summer rain eased over me, cool, through the open window in the late evening. 'Be proud,' she said. 'Even though there is a terrible war.' I lay there and listened to her. A single hard, cool star burned in the violet night – flashed and skittered as the lace edge of the curtain fluttered around it. She sat there in the dark with me and told me stories.

ooooooooooooooooooooooooooooooooooooooooooooooooooooooooooooooooooooooooooooooooooooooooooooooooooo

Dreaming of the Sun

We looked down from our rose garden eight kilometres across the low fields of weeds and abandoned fruit trees over the flat, grey fogs of the Rhine. We lived there across the river from Strasbourg, where the wind splashing east from the brick and urine of the cities sifted into the first forest trees. Back then, before the rape, before I learned to hide from the world, we used to wish that storks would nest on our roofs, even clog up the draft, because they are good luck – in spring they bring the little babies, from Africa!

Well, Africa came.

ooooooooooooooooooooooooooooooooooooooooooooooooooooooooooooooooooooooooooooooooooooooooooooooooooo

The Smell of Our Town

Our town burns in the air, and never the same twice: a rock smell, the scent of geraniums in the rain, and rotten, rain-soaked shutters; snow, four days before it falls; wildflowers; hay carted into town from the meadows in the long evening light, heat streaming down your face, coming on you as you stepped out of the church at dusk, with the first stars swaying like carp in the thick, December air; the sour smell of bulrushes, the fatty smell of soap, the sulphur of coking coal, like a violin played harshly, every note broken; the perfume of my mother's wet hair. We smelled of that.

Salvation Army 29th Thrift Store

3102 29th Ave Vernon, BC V1T 1Z1
(250) 549-4454
http://www.vernonthriftstore.ca

5/31/2016 1:44:46 PM   Dave

Books
 2 @ $1.00ea. $2.00
Senior Discount 25%   ($0.50)

TOTAL   **$1.50**
Cash $1.50
Points in this transaction: 20
Item count: 2
Trans:41007   Terminal:040103025-029001

This purchase helped someone
in your community!

ALL SALES FINAL

No Refund or Exchange
except for defective electrical
appliances over $10

You could not tell us anything.

<hr />

@ And the Cows in Their Dark Stalls

You would never think those few cows in the old streets could make so much shit. Night after night, year after year, it drained from the big timbers of the barns and rolled down the streets. The barns themselves were full of the old, fruity smell of fermented hay from the big, old, blackened beams. Walking into the barns you thought for a moment that you were walking into a meadow of flowers four hundred years ago. Time is like that. It always made me think that some day the barns were just going to float away. Instead of a town there would be only a field on the edge of the mountains, with piles of cowshit, and flowers growing out of them – daisies and lupins!

<hr />

@ I Even Found a Use for Pears

There was an espaliered pear tree against the front wall of the garage. At thinning time, I would gather up the small hard pears, hide behind the hedge, and throw them at passing cars. Sometimes I would have to wait hours – very few people had cars in those days. Sometimes I threw the pears at girls, or at old ladies walking downtown. It was not too bright, because on Sunday, when I had to sweep the street in front of our house, I would have to pick up the broken, dried-up pieces of pear. That made more work for me in the end. I can still smell the dust as I lay there behind the bushes, waiting for someone to go by.

<hr />

@ Best Friends on the Lookout

Rudi, the fruit-seller's son, and I had a trick. I would come in and tease the maids, poke them in the tits and laugh, and make jokes; he would run to the table where the maids worked, scoop up the bread they were slicing, or the sausage if there was any, and run outside with that. I would run out too, with a maid screaming and running after me! After a while there were not even sausages, and there was not much bread, and the joke was no fun at all. We still tried, but the maids would cry, because they would be beaten. We would trudge on up through the rain to Rudi's house, with maybe an onion or something, or half an onion, or a dried crust of bread, or half a dried crust of bread. The rain would grow heavier all the time, plastering us, filling the street around us, and if we tried to eat that onion our eyes would burn with tears.

❦ Night Visitors with No Time to Spare

Rudi and I would wade through the swamps of the Old Rhine – the old riverbed where the storks hunted for frogs in the rushes – looking for carp that had dug into the mud when the water burnt off. Sometimes there would be a deeper pool of clear water – like blue sky between the reeds – and the fish would be quick, like birds. In summer, big thunderstorms surged in. Thunder clouds blackened the sky and thunder boomed between the old houses like the slow, hard footsteps of the dead, who kept walking through the streets looking for their lives, knocking lightly on each door they passed by, but too impatient to wait for an answer – and afraid of one.

❦ The Mermaids of the Murg

Rain! I could tell you about rain! The rain fell so heavily in Old Town that it drained off a foot deep around your feet. One night Mama said that when the Murg floods and all the town along the river is the river, mermaids come up from the Old Rhine and swim through the streets, peering in through the windows. I never saw that. I have seen fish there. In the slow, thin, summer current of the Murg I never caught a fish, and never saw anyone catch a fish, but they swim there in the streets when the Murg floods, butting against your legs as you walk. Mama said that mermaids come to men in their sleep there. That is how they get children! They cannot get children on their own – just fish! And she laughed deep in her chest.

Cheating the Taxman

Even in the summer there were fish: salt herring in big wooden barrels in Rudi's father's store, with the paint peeling off the plaster outside – in those days you were taxed on the outward appearance of your building and a bad appearance kept your taxes low – and the floors waxed inside to a dark shine. The salt would burn my hands as I reached into the barrel.

A Smell That Would Not Rub Off the Hands

Sometimes in that old town close to the sky, I would stumble across the eel-fisher with a basket of eels that he had dragged up from the Rhine. He would go from street to street with his eels, his muddy boots, and his thick woollen workman's pants. Even in summer it was a village of water.

Sometimes I would buy eels. The eelfisher would look at me slowly out of his thin face, then reach into his basket. I never had a basket to put the eel in – I could not remember that! – so I would grab the eel in my hands and run home, the sun streaming over me like the current of a river.

The eelfisher would set his traps the night before. To reach the Rhine, he would walk down from Old Town and through our street in the dark. We would be sitting inside when we would hear the clattering of his willow-twig baskets as he went out into the fields and then down to the river. It sounded like wind, rushing away.

The smell of the eels would not wash from my hands. I would scrub and scrub with the hard soap Mama brought home from the hospital, but the cold smell of the eels would never wash off. For days afterwards my hands smelled of the willow baskets and the cold, the way a river smells of fish and fish smell of a river.

∞∞

Falling Stars

In Old Town, where Maria died on a grey horse blanket in the straw, the sky blew right down among the houses, but in the new streets where we lived in our rose garden the snow fell as a soft music. We would put down our books in the Herrenzimmer – the smoking room – leaving all our stories, and rush to the window to watch the snow fall like stars. It would be completely quiet. No sooner did the snow fall than it melted into the black soil or the cobbled streets – or it blew off and scattered through the main roads leading away from town.

∞∞

The Purpose of Stories

Der Struwwelpeter, the Scissorman, cut off children's fingers so they spurted with blood. He had long fingernails that reached to the ground. Aschenputtel, Cinderella, cleaned out the grate while her stepsisters laughed and went out dancing at big parties with lights and perfume and marble floors. Hansel and Gretel ate cookies on a Christmas house with icing dribbling down the corners so you would think it was snow. The fisherman's wife wanted to be God, and got to be, too, living in a shack made from driftwood and rocks. Schneewittchen, Snow White, had to run off to the dwarves in the forest before the queen poisoned her with an apple. To us, these were not just idle stories! They were the world.

In that winter of hunger and cold when the Swedes left our town, the snow drifted cold and brittle through the streets. Mama told us how the doors were locked under the stars, and how a darkness lay over and between the houses. She said the wolves came down from the forests that winter. I believed her, for I saw them there during the war, grey, running with the driving snow. In the morning, a washed-out, pale sun lay over everything again, as if the world had been made just then.

@ Town Weather

We always had two kinds of weather. In the new streets the rain always spat down angrily. Even if it flattened the flowers in their beds it would sink immediately into the soil. It always smelled distant, of high air and cloud, and never lasted long: it was always either going or coming. But rain to snow to sunlight, in five minutes! – the weather of the old town was a joke! We always laughed at it, chanting, 'Look! The sky is falling!' and there were always dirty, unwashed children there, with pieces of board or cut-off strips of rubber tire on their feet, ready to chase us back to our part of town under the huge white beating sails of the storks' wings. As we ran, the storks would rise at our laughter then settle back on their nests, casting giant shadows like sheets whipping on a line. To them, from their buckling potato-field coloured seas of tiles, the streets are narrow gutters under the earth. We would run wildly, laughing, over the rough cobbles, dodging the old women, maybe dancing for a second around the girls, teasing them. The young storks would clatter above us, deep in their throats, hungry for food. Sometimes I would go to Old Town to look for Rudi. The storks would be flying overhead with frogs. They would drop them sometimes, too! You had to watch out! I would find Rudi playing snooker on the lid of a garbage can set out on the street. You had to be tough to be a kid there.

@ Dreaming of Victory

Every day, with the rain drizzling itself into quiet on the new red bricks of our roof, I would stare out those round attic windows towards France as the light sang like a little girls' chorus over the fields below town. Every day in winter, in that unheated room, I would stare over the frozen grey and blue fields and over the grey fog above the black water of the Rhine and dream that we were winning the war. The eiderdown was flat by then, and the wind blew fine crystals of snow, a powder as fine as dust, into my face through the cracks around the edge of the glass.

ᐧᐧᐧ

ᐧ Complete Exposure

That is our town: the dark, yeasty streets running up through old town, the small, knotted houses, with their rooflines like the sea, like clouds, like whitecaps tearing off in storm, and the wide, paved streets below, of gardens and whitewashed houses with black shutters, open to the wind.

2. All the People of My Life

☙ Otto

When Otto was twenty, his leg was badly gored by a boar that slipped through the beaters on a hunt. After that, he walked with a terrible limp. Maybe people said they were not going to be taken in by him, but whenever he fixed his pale eyes on them, under his rough, brushy, black hair, people always bought him a beer. In the pub, he used to sweep the table clear and drag his finger through the beer stains, sketching out his ideas on the government. People soon grew tired of it, and after a while they no longer pretended not to see him on the street. They would walk right up to him as if he were an old friend from the other war, squeeze his hand hard in theirs, press some money into his palm, and walk away.

'For God's sake,' said Schmidt and Meyer when all the men drifted into their pubs on Sunday mornings to get themselves up strong for Church. 'Stop giving that old crazy man so much money! I have had enough of that war!'

Sometimes we would see men turn on their heel in the street and walk back the way they had come, or dash into an alley and slip off between houses. It did no good, all those men ducking into widow Schumacher's house to give their I am so sorry your husband died! It was just too obvious! In the end it all came back to them, for Otto played on them and always had more and more money for beer; he would spend less and less time guiding rich hunters from Frankfurt in the mountains, and more and more time shouting after us children as we played soccer in the streets: 'This is the war, boys!' He would start to laugh. 'There is no way you are going to get away from the war! There was no armistice. The people signed no armistice!'

Rudi used to stand in the goalposts, between two garbage cans he had set up in front of Franzel's barn door, and call back to him. Rudi was young, and cocky like a rooster. His eyes sparkled. He was tough. Otto must have been proud to see that. When Rudi called to him, 'Hey, Otto, when are you going to buy us men some beer!' we would laugh, grunt like a boar and kick the ball in the goal.

When Otto started knocking on doors to corner the men, they sent their wives instead. Otto looked at the women as if they were handing him all their clothes in a bundle to be given to the poor.

When the women could not stand it any more, no one in town answered their door at all.

It all came out badly in the end, for whenever a man was cornered by Otto after that he was worse off than before – Otto was always drunk by then, and so deliberately slow that he would talk even more sharply about politics. Schmidt and Meyer would stand in their doorways, wiping their hands on their aprons, looking out into the air. Whether it was hot or raining, they would stand out there, staring into the sun or the rain, looking at each other with the shouting and raised voices and clinking of glasses behind them. Someone would call for them, and they would mutter, spit onto the cobbles, and go in. It grew steadily worse.

Still, in those years of laughter when you said no to everything, there were the times you could see Otto, lonely, walking home through the rain, or just walking the streets of the town, a shadow in the shadows, drenched and cold. He looked broken, like a dropped saucer hitting the floor, breaking into long sharp splinters, broken edges of porcelain. Who knows what it means, but it means something: maybe you are going to get married too young, join the army, get shot in the guts, and die of poisoned blood, but just before you die you will see that cup, and the pattern of flowers on that cup, in the air.

Except for Papa, who had joined the party at university and was the regional doctor, Otto was the first in town to join the Brownshirts. One day he came in from Rastatt, dressed in that brown uniform with the crooked cross on the armband and that silly, narrow tie. When he knocked on a door, it opened sadly, but it opened, and the men came out in hushed tones and talked to him, while the women said to us, 'Do not talk to him, it is not easy for the ears of children.' But we did. That made them sad. Rudi asked, 'When are you going to buy me a beer, Otto?' and Otto looked at him as if he was on a star, something you could not see in the cement night.

ꙮꙮꙮ

ꙮ Maria

Maria had long black hair and skin that smelled like sunlight on a mountain. When the war began, she was ten years old, a year older than I was, with long black braids and a smile like the song of a bird, but when it ended she was alone.

∞∞

Maryushka

She was sixteen, from Nietpetrovosk. Her family had been killed by the military police. She was young and pretty, so they saved her and sent her to us. Mama was a doctor – this was the way of giving help with the children and the house. Before Maryushka came, our maids had all been young Catholic girls from town. They had been sent to us by the police, too. After Maryushka came, the house was always full of tears.

∞∞

Siegfried

Siegfried lived on Hazel Street in an old ruined house he had not cleaned for twenty years. Rats had pulled the stuffing out of the furniture, and skittered in the walls. 'Siegfried and his rats!' we would laugh. But it was not rats! When the French shells hit Siegfried's house, it exploded in a cloud of bats. They poured out of the dead air between the brick walls, up into the sun and dust and smoke like black leaves, mice skittering out into the field when you turn the hay bales over! After that, they hung in the church tower, wrapped in their wings. In the evening, they dropped out of the air and cried, close over our heads in the fields. Then they moved into our attic. To keep them out, we went up and chinked the cracks with mud and grass. They showed up all over the town. One morning I found one out the back door by the kitchen, hot and dry, like a broken leaf. I took it inside, but Maryushka screamed, 'Bats can make you sick! They will make the skin peel off your hands!' I took it outside, stretched its wings to make it fly, and threw it into the pear tree behind the garage. It landed in the weeds, so I threw it in the canal. The water closed over it, grey-green.

Then I washed my hands in the sink, and Maryushka said, 'You keep away from me!'

Siegfried was always smoking his pipe, wearing his old tweed jacket that smelled like pipe smoke. He was tanned and dark. He walked through the old town as if it belonged to him, as if he had snatched it away from God and now it was his – won it in a Skat game!

∞∞

⊛ Gossips

Gossips, eh. They always have so much to say. No one believes what they say, but they repeat it to everyone anyway: 'Schmidt's girl, Maria, she dances down at the barracks at night, and the father, he drinks too much wine, ja.' You do not know what is true and what they make up – only what can hold a person's ear becomes a story. They lived there in old town: old women without teeth; old men with their heads full of storm; weak men with their lungs burnt out by gas so they walked slowly, a wheezing like an air compressor coming down the street, as if the entire sky was sucking in and out of their lungs every time they took a step – Werner, for instance. Mama said Werner had so little lung left he must be breathing through his skin! He used to cough down once a week through the new streets to see my mama, his breath fighting in his sunken chest. They all lived there in Old Town: barefoot children dressed in worn leather pants, and pretty girls even, with big, wide, thin mouths, their blond hair crisp and brittle like straw; right up against the forest; Karl too – old Karl, with his Roman nose and the old clay pot hanging by a leather thong on a nail tapped into the plaster above his table.

In those sleepless years, even the police lived in Old Town. They never laughed. That set them apart. You could tell them a joke, but their faces would not flinch. Suddenly they would appear on Friedrichstraße, and scare us children. They liked Father Thomas's church, too, the way dogs sniff out the rabbits under the bridge footings. When they pounded on the dark doors, Father Thomas would let them in, close the door behind them, and slide the bolt.

∞∞∞

◈ Church Light

The light in the church was yellow, so broken up by passing
through the glass that nowhere was it any thicker than anywhere
else. You could thrust your hand into the light or walk through it,
yet there would be no shadow. We would be gathered around
Father Thomas, listening to him talk about his old black book.
People would come one at a time, until dirty and coughing they
filled all the pews, picking bits of wool from their sleeves. Karl
would come, pushing open the old, black, oaken doors: one carved
with the stories of Moses and Adam and Job; one with the stories
of Jesus on his Cross, and the Last Supper, dumping the tables over
in the temple, and the sheep jumping into the sea. Karl would
come in from the blue daylight to that yellow light inside the
church. Hawking into his handkerchief, turning it over in his hand
as he passed through the doorway, he would stop, inspect it carefully, then crumple the handkerchief and stuff it into his pocket.
Tante Anna would come, slow and hobbling. She would sit
amongst us children. Siegfried would come, smelling of smoke.
No matter how small or how old or weak people were they could
always push open those doors – they were perfectly balanced.
Everyone came in, shook the wind and rain out of their clothes,
and shook the sun out of their hair. Sometimes a cold wind would
blow for a moment along the floor. When the people left there was
always sawdust and straw on the pews and gravel on the floor,
skittering away from your steps – the way a crow might steal a
gold ring from you and leave a pine cone behind, something that
was worth just the same.

All the time, the yellow light hardly flickered, dimming only
slowly as the pale, watery fog-sun of that damned country of my
childhood crawled off into the forest and you could see the dark
once again through the air, then watch it replace the air. The door
would be silent, no longer opening, or banging shut. After lighting
a candle, Father Thomas would talk about his book. Even when he

finished, the words would still lie in us, like the dying, final note of a bell.

Time would be slow then. I would look around the church, in the crying, gusty shadows that bled off the candle and danced over the walls. Everyone's face would be dead and grey and would not show their thoughts as they stared ahead at Father Thomas, while I craned my head around to see *them*. One day I saw Maria was moving too. A loose hair was hanging over her face. She brushed it aside with her white hand, and it fell back again, and she brushed it back, but slowly, and shook her head. I got to know her better after that. I made a point of visiting Schmidt's inn. Maria would look up at me as I came in, and her eyes would be bright. All the old men would laugh.

Who was to know what the war would bring her in the end.

<hr />

@ The French Strategy

As Father Thomas's book slammed shut, a sudden smell of dust filled every corner and crack of the church. The light splintered and broke, and there we were, hungry, dressed in our rags, in a drab, dark room. All the time Father Thomas had been talking it had grown darker – a slow, gradual loss of light. With the slamming of the book it became pitch black. The silence echoed briefly through the room, then a low sound filled everything – the British bombers flying east over our heads. Every centimetre of the church shook with it. The world became sound. Maria was a sound in front of me, and Tante Anna was a sound, and the pews. When the police in their stiff black leather rose in the back, laughing and chatting as they slipped out the door to their posts, their voices seemed far away. You heard them across miles of fields in the night, so you did not know from which direction the sound was coming.

When they had left, after the door slammed shut, we would sit in silence. Father Thomas would blow out the candle, snuffing us all out with one puff of breath. The sound of the planes would roll over us and over us, carrying their loads to Stuttgart and Munich. A pale glow of dusk would burn in the high windows, like moonlight in the Old Rhine, chopped up, greasy and swaying, but down in the pews it would be dark. Very quietly, old Karl would tell us of the Romans fighting their way up the broad banks of the Rhine, the grey pebbles crushing under their feet in the fog. Father Thomas would raise his voice angrily, 'Yes, and the French blew up every castle along the Rhine so that the Rhine alone could keep us back – blew up every castle and killed every baron!' Karl would cut him off and tell of the gold the men wore – gold snakes coiled around their necks as they sifted through the trees against the Romans, in the forests, where you could breathe, with stars lying around in the dead leaves and the wild places, with the wolves and the boars and the deer. The Romans could not touch them there: they never left the river. Karl wanted us to be proud. He wanted us to remember that our war, which was fought to belittle us and to change our souls, to block us from love, must never, ever touch us. All the time the planes would be flying overhead and dust would shake down from the ceiling. Sometimes bits of plaster would shake loose and break up on the floor: we would all be covered with chips of plaster. We would put our hands over our heads and huddle there. Father Thomas would groan and go to fetch a broom. At the end of his story, Karl would always laugh. He would tell how Siegfried drove the Romans back, how he sacked Rome, and his men raped the women there, and we, the children, would listen, and vanish into the dark.

3. The Ancient Night

Now I am back. I lie awake in bed. It is Christmas. Maria has been dead for fifty years. I try to tell myself that there is a woman lying beside me, that I have finally made it good, I am safe, I have a big farm in Canada, grandchildren, I have returned to sign away my rights to this house, but it seems like a dream. There is only one night. It goes on forever.

After the American bombers have passed overhead, I sit in the black church. It pulses around me like a stone lung. As the sound holds in the air, I race up the tower stairs to ring the warning bell. With each toll the storks scatter from their roofs, the white of their wings the last flash of colour in the darkening town. As I pound down the steps from the tower and into the open air the first rain-drops are falling out of the near-dark. A few drunks – Otto, and his friends, and old Karl, the soapman – stagger out of Meyer's inn, squinting against the sudden darkness. Rain splashes out of the tin dragons on the gutters, splattering over my face and shoulders. The sky is heavy with storm, and the last echo of the bell hangs low and clear in the air, breaking up over the houses as it dims, like water lapping at the shore of a lake. As the silence deepens, the people sense it and slip quickly home, covering their heads from the rain.

I walk back through rose gardens and white stone fences. The houses are naked in the sky; the wrought-iron balconies have all been taken away for the war, turned into tanks and shit at Stalin-grad, oil barrels and shell-casings – along with the statue down-town, Saint Mandel, who stood on the town wall at night and sang hymns to the Swedes when they were camped in the fields. In our war, men even took the weathervanes from the barn roofs and gut-ted the old brickworks for the metal they could get out of it – the kiln carts used to run on rails, stuff like that. The stars twinkle overhead, as if they are cut out of tinfoil cigarette wrappers. As it grows increasingly dark I walk more and more slowly. The dark presses in. Some sounds carry for a long way, yet the closest sounds, my footsteps on the road or the cloth rustling on my legs, are muffled. I can hear the rusty creaking of the stars, or rocks rolling over in the bed of the river, and a man down at the hospital as Mama breaks his leg to set it again – the short, high scream.

Sometimes the sounds come through long and steady. Sometimes they are muffled and short – like a radio in the night.

∞∞

The Eternal Flood

Up in old town the rain came in floods, and flecks of straw ran down the streets. The fat woman up there, Franzel, bellowed, trying to save her cows; and the screaming of those cows! The laughter of the children too, as they pulled off their clothes and swam in front of their houses, with the water all the way up to the windows and geese swimming on it as white as clouds. Sometimes Tante Anna walked out with the children. Her huge black skirts floated around her, and she pulled the pins out of her hair. It was long and brittle, grey, and the wind caught and rustled in it. One day she started dancing and giggling in the middle of the street in the rain. The next thing, she burst out crying. She said: her young man, who had gone off to Verdun so many years before and had never returned, walked right up to her through the flood and spat in her face. All the sound of the flood and of her laughing with the children in the flood, washes down to where I walk through the clear warm rain.

∞∞

The World That Used to Be a Story

Every day the one day that is our lives grows larger. There is more and more to see, but it is between things that are already there. It is as if we grow very, very clear, and we see whole days through ourselves, and people moving, until we just vanish and only those people and those days are there. It was not always like that. In the bitter nights draining from the black heart of the forest, the starlight would drift in the streets. Dogs would scamper through it, nipping each other, tumbling over and over, barking. All the people would lean out of their windows and yell at the dogs, 'Shut up, for Christ's sake!' but they would be close to laughing, for the starlight clung to the buildings and the roofs, and the people themselves burned with a slow, white light. When the stars were at their brightest and the dogs had all been dragged back inside and were scraping at the doorways and whining, and the people yelled at them from the bedrooms upstairs then stuck their heads under their white pillows, angels would walk into town, tall and thin. Rudi saw them one night as the streets swayed in the dark like the branches of a tree. The angels nailed black crosses on each door – except the door of Stern, the tailor. That they pushed open and walked in.

Rudi did not have a clue what it meant. The next day, we went to look for footprints in the tailor's boarded-up shop. The whole place was black with charcoal. We went home again, quiet. We said nothing more to each other, for we knew that sadness well; it filled the streets of New Town – by the time the starlight fell over the shoulder of the forest, drifting like spilled flour in the wind, eddying in the corners of the houses, the light would all be gone – the whole upper town would glow, pewter, but all that flowed into our part of town was sadness. It would wear you out. Mama would lie in her bed at night, alone, crying. Maryushka would lie in her bed in the next room, with her tears. Pierre would be crumpled on his cot in the coal-room in the basement. Martha would be staring, wide-eyed, sleepless. And I would lie in bed with my terrible dreams, all tangled in the down quilt, and the wind pressing up against my window, straight up from the Rhine, the whole house between us empty and creaking.

It was the same during the day. When the sun began to rise, Old Town stood in its light, while in New Town the sun always came suddenly, and so brightly that it hurt the eyes. Mama would get up in the morning, her eyes crusted with her night tears. She would say she had had terrible dreams; the angels must have been walking through town again. All the time I thought she meant Old Town. I thought the angels walked only through Old Town and disappeared into the tailor's shop, like strange wild dogs. But it was a doorway – it opened in our street. I did not call them angels at that time. I was a boy; I did not know that there could be messages – even messages that the messengers did not understand and did not need to understand.

I would ask Mama what she had dreamed about. She would look

at me with empty, frightened eyes. She would say, 'I will tell you later, Hansel. You would not understand.'

Later she realized that was no good, in the war, and told me straight out. It was always the same dream. There was a knock on the door. When she opened it, there was nothing, only a sky full of stars, like stones in a newly ploughed field. It stank like the dusty nest of a bird. Even the stars were nothing. Even the bird-stench in the air was nothing. I looked at her and wondered why she had hidden that, because I had seen that every night.

Christ, some days I came home and there was nothing. Some days I came home and there were turnips, or beets that tasted like piss. Some days I came home and there was a rabbit, but no potatoes. Or just potatoes. Some days, in those months when all the schools were shut, I would wander through the house and through town. I would see soldiers trying to get girls to fuck with them, but never, in all I heard from Father Thomas, did I ever figure out who his God was. I never knew what he meant.

4. Holes in the World

The Silences

There were empty, silent places. Sometimes when I stepped through one it was the night. Saint Mandel was there. He broke off a piece of bread and handed it to me. It all happened so slowly, like an explosion, then I was on the other side and I had nothing in my hand. Sometimes it felt like sleep, or I was inside Father Thomas's church for a minute, only the whole church was on fire; the angels had Father Thomas by the arms. There were other angels, with rifles – they did not care about the fire. I thought, something is wrong with the angels, but there was not. There was nothing wrong with the angels at all. Then I was through. I was sweating. The wind was chill. Sometimes I was suddenly walking through clotted, falling snow, sometimes through a dark barn. There were the screams of a girl there, getting raped, and the sounds of enemy soldiers shouting 'Hurry up!'

When I came out, everyone looked at me strangely. They saw I was scared, but they did not understand it either, how could they, they did the same thing. Understanding was a terrible thing. In the town where I was born it was like pity. It was something completely cut away.

Maybe everyone does live the same things. What somebody lives everyone will, when it is time. Everything that happens has already happened and is going to happen over and over, and every time it is different, because it is just a silence, a place where the world breaks down.

The real war was fought in our minds. We were taught to disbelieve everything we saw, to plunder it, to use it. Only by *moving* could we be real. The rest was just a weakness. It was unimportant. Now it is all I have left, and I do not understand it, because it is just the silent part of a boy's life, what escaped into time, what he saw and felt and which was gone just as quickly as it came.

Beer

We used to take the train into Rastatt to go to school. There was a bar down by the tracks, a dark place of piss and rotten wood, but they had heavy beer there, sour and thick. We could get it for two cents, with the workmen and the soldiers. We would get to school drunk, but we would get to school. There was a god in that beer. He took your breath and knocked you in the back of the knees. Sometimes he was not laughing – when an army officer came in he was serious as all shit, and we would gulp our beer down quickly. The hops in it would burn the roofs of our mouths, and for a minute our eyes would go absolutely clear; we could see everything and we could understand everything. Of course we could not remember any of it! As we walked out, the officers would stick their thumbs in their mouths and suck on them. We would step into the gritty, black, early morning air, with that beer god in us, and back across the tracks, the clinkers of coal and sickly weeds and thistles, the twisted metal, the spilled oil and gas and the burnt-up barrels. Right past the workmen. The prisoners.

What I remember about that is the barkeeper. He always poured our glasses extra full. He never said a word. Then we would turn around with the beer. The whole room would be full of that god. We would see him, even in the corners, bandaged, throwing dice. He would look up, sharp and expressionless, then he would stick out his tongue at us, like something out of Carnival, with a wide grin full of teeth.

⚅ The Broken Light of God

You would find people, young women whose husbands had frozen in the birch forests outside of Moscow, sitting in the middle of the street, their arms clasped tightly around their knees, sobbing. Except for Tante Anna, nobody paid any attention. The old bitch used to hit them over the head with her broom and keep hitting them, on the back or wherever, until they got up and stumbled off. I think there was no understanding at such times. You could not link two thoughts together.

◎ The One Silence

Sometimes the silence was the night, shining in the middle of the day. The silence would sit in a doorway or in the middle of the street, and anybody who lived near it could feel the cold seeping off it. For a whole week they would not sleep. In one week they would burn up half their winter's firewood – as if an iron wind was blowing. The chimneys poured with smoke. Half the wood was green still, so it smelled as if the forest was burning. The smoke did not blow away; it just settled down among the houses.

5. An Angel of Mercy

The Lard Man

We climbed up to the forest to pick beechnuts for cooking oil, tiny little nuts you can hardly hold between your fingers. There were snails there, and mushrooms – strange, coloured blobs thrusting through the mould and fallen leaves.

In those days there was too little air for all of us to breathe! All night we had to lie in our beds totally still – not breathing – so there would be something to breathe during the day without our lungs aching and tight. Bats would not sleep as quietly as we did. We would wake up often, hungry, but we would not move.

Carrying back snails from the forest, we would see Bernd, the soapmaker, walking from door to door collecting lard. He was tall and thin, as if he stood on stilts. He knew we all used the lard, spread it on our bread and ate it like butter, but he would still walk down the street, door by door, his empty buckets clanging hollowly against each other from streets away.

Carnival Dreams

Every night for two weeks after Carnival I had a dream. In my dream everyone in town was walking together along the dusty road into the fields. Some men had long wooden noses and black hair, some people had painted their teeth black, one man was dressed as a bear, in a real bearskin. You were not sure he was not a bear – he was crazy. You had to keep away or he would crush you in his big arms and throw you in the muddy ditch as if you were a doll. There was Struwwelpeter, with awful, long, silver fingernails, and women in masks, and children dressed as animals. One woman looked exactly like a crow. She had sticks in her hand and kept hitting us children with them! There were no other people there except me. All the time the light was music tapped out on sticks of wood, not like any real sort of music – stork music. I ran ahead, the leather shorts scraping against my legs, but no matter how fast or how far I ran, the animals were always right behind me. I looked back to the town, but it was not there. I looked ahead to the fields and the hedges: there was nothing there I recognized; it was a place I had never been – wild, hot and dry, with cactuses, and withered bushes. I tripped on a hot, jagged rock and fell down into the ants. There was dust all over me.

I would wake up. The moon would be streaming in through the window – a dead moon. I never told anyone. For two weeks I never got much sleep, but I never said a word about that sad country, with the faded wooden houses. And then I moved there: Canada, where the orchards lie on the high ground along the hills, full of snakes. I moved there to get away from my dreams. You cannot get away from your dreams.

Sometimes during the day I would hear that music and I would look up, suddenly cold: there would be the storks, snapping their long orange beaks together. I would be under one of their nests. But that was then, of course. It was only the beginning. Soon there was going to be no New Town or Old Town. They are dreams, that is all they are. It is terrible. You know what is going to happen but there is nothing you can do about it, because it is all different in the world. When you dream while you are awake – well, you would think that would be an improvement, but it is worse.

∞∞

✇ The Smell of History

The hallstand had bevelled crystal, and roses carved in the dark wood. The rose leaves were elm and willow. It was Russian. Our family got it in Poland years before, when we owned the coal mines at Beuten. After he was driven out, my grandfather used to go for long walks in the mountains and read Schiller, sitting in the grass among the mountain flowers. That is how he died – with a newspaper in his pocket, in a high meadow, right after the snow had left the ground. They found him with his walking stick, a cock pheasant's feather in his cap, and a newspaper with headlines about how much money the Poles were making from their coal: Poland Rebuilds! I always thought that hallstand was my grandfather standing there. It smelled of wax from that day when he had fled to the Rhine. No matter what people did later to that hallstand, regardless what kind of wax they put on it, it always smelled of the wax the maid had rubbed into it that last morning in the East.

A Vision of God

Martha was always at church. You would think she wanted to marry Christ – or they had locked God in there and were playing checkers with him! Rudi always said, 'They have something going on in there – like dogs in the middle of the street, with Tante Anna running out, laughing and dancing around them as they pound away, and everyone else opening their windows and shouting at her to stop it, for God's sake, and laughing! If a dog could laugh it would be like that! A real cackle!'

I laughed too. 'You think,' I asked, 'He does it in the confessional box?'

'Right through the grate!' roared Rudi. 'Then the stork flaps its wings on the top of the church! You just run in next time – there is your sister, her hair all mussed up.'

'Like she has seen God?'

'Ja,' laughed Rudi. 'Then the bells ring!'

Where did he get his imagination!

Maybe all young girls like to go to church. Something white and clean, like snow or linen. They know all about linen – ironing it and pressing it.

The First Light of the World, the First Dark

In the afternoons the sun lay on the streets like a broken egg yolk – all that was left in the air was the reflected light off the ground. The wind was the shapes of the houses blowing through the air. There were scraps of shell up there – white eggshell.

Martha would walk down the street, her braided hair swinging behind her like sheaves of wheat. Sometimes Maryushka would go with her, but usually she sat in the kitchen and stared at the wall above the table or cried. We would be playing soccer. The ball would roll across the road whenever there was a goal. You would try not to allow a goal, because then you would have to run down the hill after it!

Rudi always yelled, 'Hey, there goes your sister, Hansel!'

I would just try to ignore her, so I would laugh too.

'Hey, Martha!' Rudi would shout. 'When are you going to marry me, hey?'

He shouted it in memory and he shouted it in my dreams.

Martha would just smirk and say, 'As soon as you grow up, Richy!'

We would all laugh, and the girls would go by. Sometimes Maria was with them, and Maryushka, and sometimes Tante Anna. They would slip into the door of the church. Those big dark doors would swallow them up.

oooooooooooooooooooooooooooooooooooooooooooooooooooooooooooooooooooooooooooooooooooooooooooooooooo

@ The Angel on the Other Side of the World

Papa said you could have all the stupid thoughts you liked about culture and art and love, but the reality was someone could take them away. They were nothing. They did not mean anything. They did not have anything to do with how people lived in the world, which is what you had to believe and work with. He said the world is built out of force, and without force you cannot make anything. Because of that, because she did not live for that, Martha was nearly invisible.

Martha brought flowers to all of Mama's patients in town – there were so many flowers then, as if the war had brought them forth. Nothing you could eat would grow so quickly or so well. Martha would knock gently at the doors all through the town, try-ing to hide the smile in her face, but it would break out suddenly like the sun. She would hand sick people flowers that she had picked in the fields and the hedges – lilacs and even daisies. One afternoon she walked through the smashed-up railbeds picking glorious purple thistles. She wrapped her hands in big dock leaves and carried the thistles all the way through town to Rudi's. Tante

Anna passed her and said, 'Fräulein!' My sister laughed and did a little dance, spun around. Tante Anna laughed and spun around with her. Then Martha went on, up to Rudi's. You know, I saw it all, through the lace of Rudi's window, that torn, grey, dirty lace of his mother's curtains. Rudi's mother was dead, so the curtains were all ripped. The furniture was covered with dirty things, boots and cups, and was stained with soup. The chairs had lions' feet on the bottom of the legs! Rudi's dad drank too much.

He said, 'Rudi, you clean up.'

But Rudi did not. His dad must have been blind to it, I do not know, but there it was, he did not see it or he did not say anything, so it never got cleaned up.

'Maybe that is why you are sick,' I said to Rudi. 'You need a maid.'

'Only doctors get maids,' Rudi snapped back.

Ja. So I said, 'Maybe you need a girlfriend.'

'Who in this town,' he said. Ja.

I was looking out the window. There came my sister, laughing, with a huge stupid bunch of thistles like a big broom in her hand. She came right up to the door! Her knock echoed hollowly through the house.

Rudi said, 'Come in here!'

Martha opened the door. When the door was open, the light poured in and the thistles burned before her, but when it closed she was in shadow, dim and grey. The smell of those thistles flooded the room. It smelled like we were living in a thistle down by the tracks, blind and hot with the sun so you could not stand it.

'I heard you were sick,' Martha said. 'Here are some flowers.' She saw me and she blushed. 'Roses!' she spluttered, and slipped out the door again. Rudi turned to me, smiling. He was holding the flowers in front of his chest. As Martha slipped out, her skirts brushed against the doorframe and rustled like wind in trees. When the door was open, Rudi's face was speckled and blotched with colours from the thistles as the light shot through them and over his face; when the door closed it was as if night had suddenly swept over him.

In the grey, thin light, Rudi dropped the thistles and swore because they pricked his hands. He looked up at me with a crazy, hurt, empty look, his face as dark as charcoal in that shadow – confused, as if for once he did not know what was going on, as if I was a door you kick at so the old man opens up inside and you run away down the street laughing. The old ladies come to Mama later and say, 'Oh, that Hansel, he's trouble, those boys he's with up there in Old Town!' and Mama says, 'Yes, yes, Tante,' and closes the door, looks me squarely in the face, then bursts out laughing, and shakes her head. She must have seen the silence, too. Rudi looked at me like that. But he did not laugh.

'Come on, Hans,' he said. 'Let's go out.'

We left the thistles lying on the floor. Every time we went in after that we just stepped beside them. After months they got crushed up into little crumbs and ground into the rug.

∞∞

Cows

Cows like to eat flowers, the petals and stems dangling out of their mouths as they stand in the fields and look at you stupidly, or in their stalls as you and Franzel fork hay into their cribs. First, they push their noses through the hay and lick up all the flowers. Their tongues are rough and can scrape your skin like an old fencepost, but they can pick the littlest thing out of the hay, and daisies. They would never eat the thistles. The thistles would always be lying there when they had finished. The cows would eat everything else – all the grass, the dandelions and cowslips and buttercups, mustard, vetch, bitter mustard, and wild lettuce, even though it is as prickly as thistles, and wild carrots, even dill. They would be so cheerful. Their whole bony flanks would tremble; they would slap their tails at flies, happily, eating the flowers.

6. A Woman Alone

A World of Women

We lived in a world of women. Most men we saw were insane, or stumbling on butchered legs down the street. Men wore uniforms, carried guns, and were either extremely polite or sneering, but they had left our world. The women were alone. There were old men, of course, laughing and spilling their beer on their cards, really splurging and eating sausages if Schmidt had them for once, or at Meyer's, if Meyer had them, and Otto's voice the loudest of all. All the other men had walked away. The women stayed behind, afraid. They could see everything changing, because they were not walking: they were just standing still, like trees, with roots.

Cobwebs

The hard, cold, black-grouted, white tiles of the kitchen flowed up to the ceiling. In the morning the spider webs on the ceiling would catch the light trickling in through the window, and would look like stars. When Mama came home from the hospital, I always heard her say to Maryushka, 'Clean up the cobwebs tomorrow, Maryushka,' but Maryushka never did. Mama never said a thing about it. Every day she simply told Maryushka to sweep them down, and every day they grew bigger. I wonder what Mama thought of them there – she never saw Maryushka in the morning, sitting at the small table in the corner, looking up at them as if there was nothing else around her. With the blackout shutters closed to the garden. In the grimy light.

The Genius

Michel wanted to make a model of the church for school. He had me climb up to the high, stained-glass windows of the church and measure everything to the last millimetre. He stood far down below, and wrote it all down. Then he went home and built the church absolutely to scale. He had me climbing all over that church for a month. It was very dangerous. I hated him for it.

∞∞∞

@ I Learned Proper Table Manners

We had to sit upright with a book under each arm. You had to squeeze the book tightly or it would fall. You could not let it fall. You had to hold the fork in your left hand and the knife in your right, and never change hands. You had to lift the food to your mouth, not lower your mouth to your food. If it was soup, you could bend over just a little. There had to be a fresh tablecloth for every meal. When I first came to Canada and there was no damask tablecloth on the table, only a piece of oilcloth, and there was no china or silver, and no crystal, I thought I would die; I thought I would never be able to survive here, but I did. I learned quickly what was important.

∞∞∞

@ Escape through the Rose Garden

We dug a tunnel every night for five weeks in the second winter of the war. The maids got off work at 8:30, put us all to bed in our pyjamas – six kids from four to fourteen years old – locked the doors and left. Once we were sure they had gone, we tied our sheets to the window and climbed down. Michel said, 'There is a dirt floor in the wine cellar and there is our sandbox by the canal. We can have a secret entrance!'

Night after night, we slipped out in our pyjamas. We dug thirty metres before we gave up. Michel dropped the project as quickly as he had picked it up. It was ridiculous. We hardly got any sleep.

We had a lot of sand and nowhere to put it, so we threw it in the canal, laid boards over the hole, and covered them with sand. One day we stood there with the mayor and the firemen, looking at the dam in the canal as if we had never seen it before in our lives. It was awfully funny. They said, 'Frau Doktor,' very politely when Mama came, and nodded gravely. The dirt we had dug out of the tunnel completely blocked the canal. No one could figure out where it had come from. There was no evidence of it at all.

At least Michel thought of wooden supports, so the whole stupid thing did not fall down on our heads. We got the wood from the bombed-out school across the canal. Michel laughed, 'We can steal the door off the garage!' Mama never knew! She came home late at night and left early in the morning and she did not have a car. We carried that big plank door through the rose bushes, and threw it into the canal with a big splash. Then we all splashed through the water in our pyjamas under that big weeping willow, climbed onto the raft, and pushed across. We were like Huck Finn on the Mississippi.

Four weeks later, the maid said Papa was coming home on leave. Right away, we ran straight down to the canal and got that door! The bad water in the canal had wrecked all the paint, but we hung the door back on the garage anyway. That evening in the dusk Papa came home in his black car. Michel said, 'He's here,' and we all ran to the windows. What I saw that night I will never forget, because there was Papa standing in front of the garage door, looking very puzzled. We could tell right then he was not going to be mad. It was just something he did not understand. One half of the door was white and clean, new and shining in the last light; the other half was grey and peeling – and wet! Papa stood there for a few minutes, then he came in, and he never said a thing about it, ever.

◇◇

◉ My Parents

Papa sat at the piano in the Herrenzimmer and played the Pathétique Concerto. We did not dare go in. He played and he played until Mama came home, late. We lay upstairs, afraid, in the white moonlight, picking the sand from under our fingernails, and listened to that music. It was the first night in weeks we had not been out working on the tunnel. We heard Mama downstairs talking to Papa. Shit, what were they talking about. We all heard it plain enough, but what did it mean?

'I work seventy-two hours without a break. I take drugs to keep me awake. Some kid comes in and I have to decide whether he should live or not as he is bleeding on my table. They have no right to talk about planning. I am going to get killed too. How could you do that to me, Martha? How could you send me there?'

'You were having an affair. I did not know there was going to be a war.'

'Then you are stupid.'

And a door slammed.

After that I just heard Mama crying. We all heard that. It pooled and echoed in the whole house. It was a house of tears. What is that supposed to mean? We did not know what we were supposed to do, so we did nothing.

∞∞

◎ Our Private War

The truth is, it was our war. The war was as much between Mama and Papa as it was with England and Russia. Most of the time it was just fought with silence and absence. Papa was in his field hospital, on the front. Mama was looking after the hospital in Rastatt.

Papa left the next morning. He closed the door of the garage tightly behind him and gave each of the girls a hug and shook our hands, the boys. He said nothing to Mama. We heard him shifting the gears of his car on those dirt streets through town, then out into the fields. When it was silent, Mama sat us down on the steps and told us a story.

'After the Swedes surrounded our town, Wallenstein was up in Ebersteinburg, the robber castle. The knights could see all the roads leading through the forests and down into the plain, and used to ride down and steal gold from travellers. When Wallenstein was caught up there, the Swedes had already knocked off the tower and blasted half of the walls apart. All the wooden roofs and the wooden walkways were burning. The Swedes thought they had finally captured Wallenstein, who had been causing them so much trouble in this part of the country, but as they watched he leapt with his big, white stallion off the edge of the burning castle into the steep, dark ravine. The Swedes went down right away. It took them hours to force their way through the thorny underbrush, but they never found any sign of Wallenstein, or of his white stallion. Do not forget that: you live in a country of magic, where a man can disappear. When nothing else will make things happen, magic may, if you believe in it.'

A Party in the Rose Garden

And a week later, Frau Sturmann fell into our tunnel! It was terrible. Mama was having a party, the last garden party she would have before the war took over all our lives and squeezed us out of those places where we used to live. The guests were party officials, businessmen, local politicians. Frau Sturmann was a very stuck-up old lady, but she was Mama's friend. Mama was very busy as the hostess. There were people in all the rooms of the house, and people walking around, laughing loudly. The men sat in the Herrenzimmer and smoked cigars. The stinking grey smoke settled to the floor and around their feet. Mama said to Frau Sturmann, 'Frau Sturmann, I am so glad you could come. Let us go out into the garden for a moment so we can be alone and talk.'

We did not know anything had happened until we heard the screaming. We ran outside. There was Frau Sturmann, alright. Only her head and shoulders were sticking up above the ground. She was not the nice old lady any more. Mama was trying to help her out of the ground, but Frau Sturmann was screaming at her that she was crazy and her whole house was crazy and her kids were worse than dogs! Michel and I ran out and pulled her from that hole. She was stuck very badly, as if she was planted there. She came out with her dress covered with sand and dust. That was really something for an old lady! By this time everyone from the party was leaning over the railing at the back of the house and looking down into the rose garden.

'That is it! You are a stupid woman and your husband does not

love you, and I will never, ever, see you again!'
She stormed off.

Once she was gone, Mama looked up at the house. Everyone was staring at her, without saying a thing. As Michel and I watched, Mama walked through the garden, picking a few roses. When she had a handful, she walked into the kitchen and set them in a bowl, went into the dining room and told everyone they had to go home. The evening light came in long, slanting yellow beams through the west windows and splashed across the floor, throwing long, dark shadows. Everyone stepped through those shadows and those beams of light. They all flickered like the leaves on a birch tree in the forest, turning over and under in a light wind.

Some of the people said they were sorry, but many of them did not. Mama knew right away which ones were going to speak to her again and which ones were not. When you are a kid, you know which people are your friends and which ones are your enemies, but when you are grown up, when you are a certain kind of grown-up like my mother, you think you can get somewhere with people by talking to them or by doing good things or by being polite, but it is not true; any child could tell you that: some people are your enemies and they wish you nothing good. The loss of society was hard for Mama, later, with the blackout shutters closed, listening to the Canadian planes flying east high overhead, and the booming of the flak guns along the Rhine.

She called us inside that night, and asked if we knew anything about the hole in the garden. Naturally, we said, 'No, we do not know anything!' Then Mama laughed. She laughed till the tears came to her eyes like raindrops and she wiped them off with the knuckles of her hand and they came again.

'Just there with only her head and shoulders sticking up out of the ground! Ha! The stupid old woman. That is just what she deserved! Meddling in other people's business!'

No one came to the house again. Mama was alone. Every night, she came home later and later from the hospital.

Letters came from Sebastopol, or Salonika, or Marrakesh. When the men came home on leave, they could not stand to be with their wives. After a couple of days they had to return on the train – they would climb back into the cars almost with relief. But it was not relief: it was as if they were already dead. They were not men any more, not people like us any more. All us children wanted to go on those trains with them, for there were two worlds and ours was only a shadow. Papa's big picture of our Leader still hung in the front hall, above the rosewood hallstand, but no one saw it any more. We were all so used to it being there that it had become invisible, and there never was anyone other than us there to see it.

The war was claiming Mama more and more as well. If I wanted to see her, I had to get up at 4:30 to walk with her to Rastatt, down by the Rhine, five miles through the fields of old fruit trees and high grass. The night smelled of sulphur from the coking coal we burnt. When we got farther out into the fields, the darkness turned into fog, and when the sun rose it surrounded us; the whole world was white. As we walked out into it we could hear the dogs barking at the prisoners' camp. In that fog, the sound of barking seemed right beside us as we walked. Every morning, Mama told me stories, and every morning the moans of the sick men in the Rastatt Hospital ran to us across the fields and jumped up on us and licked our hands. We just had to ignore it, just had to pretend it was not there, until suddenly we were walking into the edge of the city, among broken, burnt buildings.

7. Our Wooden Christ

@ What We See

You are used to thinking a story starts in one place and goes into another place, and there is only one place it can go. When someone tells a story you see each part of the story one after another and cannot see the end until it is over, but when you hear a story a second time you know how something that is said or something that is done in the first words is already telling you what is going to happen at the end. In the same way, we pass along life to those who come after us, but we also pass along death. How are you going to make a country out of that? I thought I could get away from that accursed land of my childhood. There is no such thing as justice or pity among people, only ideas of justice and pity. Sometimes you see those ideas and sometimes you see what there is among people. We are like transparent panes of glass. We walk through the streets of Rastatt, five hundred years old; the wind blows through the glass and whole centuries shine there until a cloud passes over the sun; then they are gone and when the cloud has passed a completely different life is there, a completely different person.

@ What Mama Said While the Dogs Barked

'When you were born, Hansel, you were very sick. You could not drink milk at all. We were living at the university in Freiburg. We gave you cognac. You lived on that for two weeks. It saved your life! After that you were such a happy baby! We were very poor. It was a difficult time. Your father joined the party and the students' organizations, but he still did not get in to teach at the university. He was not good enough for that, even as a party man.'

@ What Mama Said As We Walked through the Ruins

'The worst thing about our time is everything is becoming invisible; every day there is a little less of us that can see and talk about things – the parts of our lives that used to be so important, that used to be where we lived, are becoming invisible, and we cannot use them any more. All the stories are dying. There once were stories about all the towns in this area. People used to gather to tell them, because they used to be part of them. Now the stories are stronger than we are. They are not human stories any more. That is why I tell you stories, Hansel: so I can remember who I am and someday maybe there will be something there to help you remember who you are, because everything is working to make us invisible, to eliminate people from the world and for there to be something else in their place.'

∞∞∞

✾ Father Thomas

Father Thomas used to lay his black book, with its old, heavily carved letters, on his lap and smooth the pages down with his long, white fingers. It smelled of shoe leather and mildew. Young women who wanted to get pregnant would try to touch that book, and we boys would try to get a good smell of it – that was supposed to be lucky: you could not get shot up in the war if you got a smell of that book right down into the bottom of your lungs!

Years before, Papa had hung a picture of our Leader beside the cross, behind the altar – crusted with gold flowers and angels. As Father Thomas came in one day, he found the wooden Christ – with all his loud blue paint and the red paint for blood – broken off the black wood of the cross at the hands and feet, and our Leader nailed to the cross in its place with one nail, driven right through the glass. Long knives of glass lay on the floor. Our Leader had a terrible, stony expression on his face. It was frightening. I saw Rudi later. 'Hansel!' he laughed. 'You should see the picture down in the post office! Crying like that statue of Mary down in Göttingen!' Rudi took me down to see it. The picture really was crying. To touch it, people had come from all around. Word spreads fast. Our Leader looked confused. There was blood trickling down from between his eyes, as if he had been shot.

After that, we went through the whole town. The pictures had all changed. The one right inside the door of Meyer's pub had turned a beautiful shining blue, as if it had become water. We went across the street to Schmidt's. The picture above the bar had clenched its eyes shut. There was the shadow of an eagle over it. Immediately, we ran down to the mayor's office, and burst in through the door. There was the best picture yet! It was smiling. It was not a sort of smile that would make you happy. It was awful. He did not know how to smile, somebody had told him about it, about smiling and how lovers do it sometimes, and children too, so he tried it and it was like bent wire – get it caught in the spokes of your bike.

Father Thomas thanked God he did not have a tall, pretty steeple, with gold, and with rose petals carved in the corners, just a short, thick one to hold that big bell we had – the biggest bell in the whole area. The date was cast in there at the foundry when they made it, 1621, so it was old. The steeple was hidden by the slope. The enemy could not sight their guns on it.

With a broom of birch twigs from the forest, Father Thomas swept around our Christ. He looked very small on the floor. Flashes of dust flew into the air from the broom as the walls of the church began to vibrate from the traffic. When Father Thomas had cleared away all the glass he picked up our little God in one hand the way a little girl picks up a doll; with his other hand he grabbed our Leader off the wall. He walked through the drumming hall of the church, with the dust hanging yellow in the air, into the tower. The calls of the baby swallows echoed down from the roof, the rope hanging perfectly still beside him, as if it were dead, or on fire, straight and steady down from God. In the tower, Father Thomas set our Christ and our Leader on to the floor. Whenever I rang the bell after that, I stood on a pile of old junk – empty wine bottles, that the soldiers had found and finished off one night, all the hymn books, stacked up because we were not supposed to use them any more, the swallows, the bats – sleeping – and little white piles of swallowshit and batshit. There were clots of mud all over the books! The swallows would be flying in and out with food for their babies. On the top of the junk was that broken Christ and our Leader, staring at me.

A Premonition

The first time the French shelled our town all they managed to blow up was the school across the canal from our house. A huge shell came over at the beginning of the war, weeping through the air like a pack of angels. We all cheered! That night I had a dream. There were angels around the school, dressed in black. Some of them were going through the ruins with flashlights, picking up books. They laughed and threw all the books in a pile, and poured gasoline over them. The fires gave off sooty, black smoke that you only knew was there because there were no stars, only sometimes a star, sometimes one or two stars. When the fires were blazing strongly, the angels slammed into their trucks, their headlights still dimmed, and drove downtown, but they never got downtown. I heard a knock on our door: they were there, parked in the yard, pounding at the door with the butts of their rifles, and yelling, 'Open up, for God's sake!' There was not even any starlight. I could not see in the house. I waited for Mama to go to the door, but she did not, she had not heard it, so I went down, my footsteps booming on the stairs. The door was open. Outside, it was a strange country: flat fields, grain fields to the horizon, the sky above it, as if I was living in the sky, as if that was the proper place to live – I was a creature of the sky, like a bird. When I went back into the house there were drifts of dust in all the rooms, like snowdrifts. I slipped back into bed. The roof had been blown off by a shell. And still no one else had woken up! The dust rose off the bedsheets as I crawled in, and I coughed and coughed and coughed.

The next morning there was no hole in the roof. I lay there all night with the smoke blowing away and the stars gradually forming like gold sinking in the deep pools of a river and burning above my face, but when the morning came it was all gone. I could hear Maryushka clanking around in the kitchen. I got up and went down. Maryushka gave me a couple of dried apple slices. That is what I had to eat. I went outside and the sun was shining, and it was real.

The Single Choice in the Single Dream

Dreams are not just something we do. They are all around us. We share them so we remember the dead and they remember us, in the same dream.

It is the worst thing in the world. They give you a broom and say, 'Sweep the streets!' Why in the hell you should do it, you do not know, because in the end it does not make any difference if you sweep the streets or not. You have to choose between washing your hands and washing your hands. You let the water pour over them out of the tap. It is cold. It smells of the mountains. Or you let the water pour out of the tap. It is cold. It smells of the mountains. It is terrible. You just cannot choose like that. The snow swirls around you in the street or the snow swirls around you in the street. All you can see is white and the shadows of the houses, as if they were a fire that died down a long time ago. You have to choose between your dreams. *One* of them is real – but only if you will it to be real. Your dreams are all around you, but you can only find them in your memory; the sun is too bright – it makes every day look different. What you remember of your dreams makes no sense – God has already left. He is always leaving. You know He is there because He has left. When you have Him in front of you, you do not know it. Choice was something missing in us – something had broken.

8. Prisoner of Circumstance

Maryushka was always washing herself in the sink. Whenever Mama came home she would sigh, but she would never say anything. Maryushka seemed to be clean enough. She never smelled of sweat or onions, but she was always washing, as if she was trying to wash the smell of the hospital soap off her hands with the soap, or the smell of the water with the water so she would smell of the soap.

When Bernd came looking for lard, Maryushka was leaning against the kitchen wall – laughing. Pierre was at the table, his bandages loose on the table, dark and stained – Mama's old wedding sheets torn up into strips. Pierre dabbed at his head with a wet cloth, dipping it into a bowl of water. His leg was unbandaged, shrivelled and weak, propped up on another chair. Pierre. What was he doing here. I turned to Martha. She was afraid; her eyes burned with hate and confusion. As Bernd swung into the kitchen she saw the shock on my face; I could read it in her eyes.

When he came, Pierre was wearing thin cotton clothes from the camp. He was bleeding. Maryushka pulled him inside. I knew at once that he was from that camp out in the old wheat fields, where the dogs would bark at us and jump up against the wire mesh when we went by. Rudi always used to say: 'Well, if they got out they would eat you!'

Then I could not hear my heart. I could not hear anything, not even the slates creaking in the attic as a cloud went between the house and the sun. Bernd was there in the kitchen, with his lye-burnt hands. His fingers were like roots, like foam as the wind blows upriver in the flood. If anybody knew about Pierre, it meant death to us all. There was no one you could trust. We were all prisoners. You have to hide the good things you try to do, but maybe they do not always turn out to be good, because the world is not good.

Bernd nodded sharply at Pierre and hardly glanced at Maryushka. He thumped his hand on my shoulder and in a cracked voice asked for lard. His voice was like a geranium pot that had smashed and broken on the street. Like a puppet on strings, I took him through the kitchen, opened the cupboards one at a time and banged them shut loudly with my anger, each one louder than the last, trying to get him out of there. In each cupboard there was nothing: no lard, no tins of beans, no meat cans, no salt fish, no sauerkraut, no flour, no sugar, no canned pears, no potatoes, no onions, no canned tomatoes, no pepper, no oil. Bernd began to laugh, a thin old man's laugh. Damn it, what did he know that I did not! The next cupboard I tried to open, he held shut with his fist. I pulled on it, but he was stronger and held it shut. He pushed laughing out the back door into the garden and the September night. A few dried leaves blew in the door. All the time Maryushka was over the sink, washing onions, peeling off their thin brown skins, slipping the mildewed skins into her mouth and chewing on them.

I burned with shame. I turned around, red-faced, and Pierre was laughing at me through his bandages. Martha pushed him out of the room. The hall door banged shut on its springs behind him, slowly flapped back and forth in the doorway until Martha backed up against it with her hip and it stopped.

'What in the hell do you think you are doing bringing him in here? Do you think the police like people who hide prisoners in their basements? Do you think that is why we have the police, for Christ's sake?'

I looked up at her with one scared glance, then raced out the back door into the night, trying to catch Bernd, my breath pounding and my thoughts pounding with it. The dark leapt up over me like a flame.

❦ The Wounded at Night

At night, the men who had been shot up drank their sleep out of a glass of water the nurses handed to them. Sleep sat smiling at the foot of each bed in turn. She had some flowers that she had picked in the ditch, and left one on each bed. You could not wash the smell of those flowers away. Even the nurses smelled of it. It got into their clothes and their skin. They washed and washed, but only polished it up or moved it around – they did not wash it off. Of course, the soap was not any good for that – thick, greasy, brown cakes that looked like a skin disease. The smell of the flowers was all through the hospital, filled up with all those men sent back. All night their ghost limbs, lost arms and legs and their broken-up brains – like the glass inside a thermos, when you smash it – rustled under the sheets, groped around trying to find ghost bodies to fit onto. You cannot tell the world from what you think of the world when you look at it.

<hr/>

@ Papa's Soul

I am back and am unable to sleep – I am afraid of what I am going to say in the morning; I am going to say something no-one wants to hear.

Papa always said Beethoven was his soul, as no other music was.

'Do not talk to me about this damned soul,' said Blaumann, walking on the old Roman road up through the Black Forest, as we were looking for berries. 'Just think of all the horrors that have been committed because of that soul. Do not talk to me about it!'

<hr/>

@ Candle Stubs

Our Christmases were terrible. When Papa was in Russia he came home for a couple of days, but he was not the same man any more. We had a tree, and Mama had managed to save a few candle stubs. We could only light them once, that is all we had. There were no presents under the tree, not even for the little kids. There was nothing to eat. It was awful. We all cried.

<hr/>

@ The Brickworks

I went to the old brickworks once, with the storks flapping up and sitting on that tall smokestack. Inside, there were costumes for

Carnival, in storage. Once I put on an angel mask – a bird mask, with a person's pale face, with pink smudges on the cheeks. When I looked out, all the other costumes were alive. They were laughing! They looked up at me as if I was a wild thing that had just run out of the forest into the firelight. They did not know what to do. It went totally silent. The laughter stopped. An old man stood up. He looked at all the others there. You could tell he was plastered. He was red in the face, and he slurred his words out slowly. He turned to the others, all the angels and devils, bears, the couple of Romans – there was even a witch there, laughing, with old wrinkled breasts, scratching at her tits! He looked at them. 'It is alright. Just be quiet.' He was talking in English. Ja, English! But I understood it! 'Go to Canada,' he said to me. 'There are mountains as tall as clouds and trees older than this town. When the trees die, people just leave them there to rot into the ground. There are wheat fields as big as the sky. This is not your country.'

I was scared, and pulled off the mask. The scene was all gone. The people had vanished. There was only a pile of masks on the floor. There was a mask on the floor where the man had been standing. The devil's mask! I put the angel mask on quickly again, but there was nothing, only a lot of crows smashing at the skylights.

⚬⚬⚬

❦ Every House Alone, Every House Alive

There were charged houses all over town, as if there were all these different towns in the same place. In some of the houses it was always snowing. In some it was always half an hour before dinnertime: everybody was grumpy, and they kept wandering into the kitchen and being sent out again, with a rap on the knuckles from a wooden spoon! In some of the houses there was nothing but smoke; fires were breaking out everywhere. It was just terrible. But that was the town: people lived there, they made do. Somehow they got on with their lives.

9. The Protecting Night

Conking Them Out

At school we got points for bringing in old cigarette wrappers, old nails, twisted bits of wire crusted with rust we found in the fields, and old tin cans. They were all melted down, cast, and dropped on London. Every day, trucks would bring junk over from France: statues – cherubs pissing water! – all jumbled together on the trucks, with twisted-up metal from old factories, and old bicycles. Once there was an entire truckload of garbage cans! It all came over the river and all of it was dropped on England, trying to conk them out. The workers came in striped clothes, barefoot. They unscrewed the numbers from our front door, cut off the iron railing from the yard, their torches sparking and leaving sharp edges where the iron melted. It burned their feet. One of the prisoners sneered at us children as we came out.

He said, 'You do not need that when you children grow up.'

We thought he was crazy.

The New Bicycle

I was looking for Bernd. The dark was looking for someone. Before it found Maria and before it found the Moroccans, it found me.

'Shit,' I called out. The blood was soaking through my pants onto my fingers. 'Shit.'

'You have wrecked my bike!' Rudi yelled. 'Look at it!'

'Where in the hell did you get a bike?' It was half dark and there were clouds, so there was not much light and I could not see clearly. I looked at it more closely. 'Where in the hell did you get a *new* bike?'

'I don't care if it is new! You've smashed it!'

'They are made out of steel!'

'Look where you're going!'

'There is a guy on a bike and a guy on his feet – it is the guy on the bike who ran into him!'

Ja, right.

But he was not listening. He was trying to fix his bike – where it lay on the street. The fender was bent up, and rubbed the wheel. So I twisted it, trying to straighten it.

'Try that,' I said.

He snatched it up and rode away, banging over the cobbles, with the fender clattering and the wheel wobbling. The last sunlight was dimming in the air, coals dying out to ashes, just flaring up once in a while when there was a gust of wind.

It was growing dark; night was gathering in the trees. How Rudi had got any kind of bicycle at all just blew past me completely. Maybe he got it from the police! The fender was making a lot of noise, scraping like a child sucking on a loose tooth. But there was no use standing there in the middle of the street, crouched under the stars, calling out at him, and I did not. He was moving away.

∞∞∞

⊛ The One Thing That Was Clear

God has a little iron hook on the end of a long long line, and it is dangling down through the air. It is covered with gold. It sparkles.

When I would ring the bell for the all-clear, relief would rise through my hands into the rope as I pulled. I really hung on that rope, and through the rope onto the bell, and I rose out through it. All the bells from the other villages came in, Grauenheim and Hinterinseln and Winterheim, and Hühnelingen, with the mulberries that looked like peacock's eyes planted all down the main street, all singing together, the small, tinny bell from Frohheim, like a sparrow, the bell from Himmeldach – a girl taking off her clothes in a hurry and she forgot to close the curtains! – the heavy, liquorice bell from Schwarzheim and the cracked bell from Weibesruck, that sounded like someone took a sledgehammer and smashed an anvil. It was such a rough bell that it hurt your ears. All those bells would be singing when they got together, as children were ringing them too – flying on them. The whole thing would get louder, and the whole air would shake.

It was as if God had a rope, and he was yanking on it, and the town was crying! You would feel it! You would rise up with it as the bell grabbed you, and yanked on you and you rose with it.

<hr />

❦ What You Do Not See Can Still Hurt You

You do not see angels going around with a bucket of glue, a mop and a bunch of handbills, plastering them on the wall: 'You Cannot Have a Bicycle'; 'God Is Not Making Any More Bicycles – God Has Guns to Make with the Steel.' What happens here is what happens with God; what happens with God happens here. It is *our* war. We have melted all our bicycles down and dropped them on London. There are many children there who do not have a mom because of our bicycles falling from the sky. It rains bicycles. The sky was so choked up with bicycles that they start to rain, a hard, hard rain!

So, you know, if bicycles can fall out of the sky, then, sure, they can just be there all of a sudden outside Rudi's door.

Time is just like a wire, off a spool: you can pull it straight, but as soon as you let go it whips right back. I stood there in the dark of Old Town, that breathing dark, with the stink around me, and the strange sound on the roofs of smoke sifting up beside the storks, crackling out of the chimney pots, and the nests snapping as the storks shifted, bits of sticks falling into the street and the storks hunching their heads from the wind that blew over the roofs. Wind did not blow in the streets, though – it would only do that at the end of the war, when the starlight thickened and began to flow down between the houses, silvering the doorknobs as it passed and lying on the cobbles like chips of sawdust on the surface of a canal – floating away, but so light that the water could not carry them and they just danced, and all the time the wind raged overhead.

<hr />

❦ Invisible

As I stood in the dark of Old Town on that terrible dusk when the world came together and God saw me for a moment, Tante Anna came up to me, white and pasty-faced like the moon. There was a shadow standing right beside me. They taught us in school that a shadow is formed when something blocks the light, but that is just what you learn in school. This was breathing. It had stinking breath. Tante Anna grabbed me by the arm, and hissed, dug her fingernails in, and made something of me, though I did not know that. She was able for a moment to make me so nobody could see me. I was invisible.

'Hansel,' said Tante. 'You need to clean your house.'

The night was pooled in her eyes – black flames, like smoke that was burning.

'Go to Thomas. He has wine. He knows what bottle. Make him give it. You are always going to him at night, so no one will stop you. If they stop you, say that you are going to the Father. But they will not. Run. No one will see you. You can run and run and no one will see you. They will look out their windows, they will see the street – but they will not see you. Go! Bring the wine to your house!'

ooooooooooooooooooooooooooooooooooooooooooooooooooooooooooooooooooooooooooooooooooooooooooooooo

❦ The Police Raid the House

And so, the black night, that old and stinking night that smelled of cows and stone and hay, wrapped itself around all of us. When the police came they did not find us, only Mama's empty house. All the sheets were on the bed, there was no soap, no blood, nothing they could smell. The police only found the table set for dinner with the best damask linen and the Dresden china, thin as a leaf, that you could almost see through. There was no food in the house. Maryushka stood in the kitchen, trying to arrange some flowers in a vase. The police did not care about her. She was theirs already! They could fuck her or make her kiss them, so she was nothing to them. They did not have to worry about her – they could come and grab her any time. As she cried, working, with the tears flowing down, they laughed, and patted her on the ass. She pushed them off and they laughed again. 'What is the matter, sweetheart!' said one of them. 'You should come down and see us in the evening! You could dance.' They dragged their dogs out by leashes wrapped

around their throats. Their boots echoed hollowly down the hall
until the door boomed behind them.

<hr>

❦ How Things Happen, How We Think,
How We Do Not Know

Some things you know nothing about. They come together or
break apart without you. After the Murg dam was blown up by the
dive-bombers, the lower part of town down by the train station was
a lake, with long, shallow waves. A huge tree sat in front of the
train station for three days, before anyone could get to it and cut it
up. Its leaves wilted, and hung down, limp and brittle. The sun
filled the whole of the air. When you walked through the air, you
were walking through the sun. Up in the old town the rats were
excited, scurrying in the walls – they could smell the water. You
got to thinking, and then something else happened and you
thought, whatever it was it did not matter, you just had to forget it,
because things happen, and that is something you know nothing
about. That is what you thought.

<hr>

❦ Shadows in Time

The faster I ran, the more slowly I went and the harder my breath
came. I saw people standing in the deep shadows of the doorways,
but they were not people – they had masks on, bear heads and
wooden masks. They stepped out of doorways and watched. I
turned and began to run through the thicker shadows along the
walls, with the moonlight lying like snow on the roofs above me.
The church looked on fire in the moonlight, standing in the square
without a shadow on it. It was white as fish-scales. There were thin
wisps of shadows, not the swallowed river of shadow I had followed out of Old Town, a river that did not move – only I had
moved! As I came out of the current and saw that fish church,
everything else was still and dark. It did not have any time any

more. It did not break off anywhere – it just stopped. I heard my breath, loud.

That was the moment the war found me. The shadows flickered over the cobbles and flashed on the walls, whipping through the air. They funnelled up over the church, like birds wheeling in big flocks over a field! The smoke was alive – thin shadows of smoke blew slowly out of the roofs. In the moonlight, shadows lay around the sharp edges of the square, curled and crumpled up over the hard corners of buildings, off the church, right up to the dark doors. I ran. Oh shit. I ran right through that smoke and pushed in through the big wooden doors without anyone seeing me.

A thin light came in the windows like a wind. It did not soak colour from the glass but was all one colour: huge blocks and squares of light, the same pale, washing-water colour as the cobbles around the fountain, as smoke from the roofs in the moonlight, as the silver combs in my sister's hair. When I moved through it, I moved through all those things, and they shifted behind me, so the past disappeared and the paths I did not choose vanished. In this way our lives seem inevitable.

Once I banged the door shut I was alone with the world. The light did not even ripple. It was as if the moon was there, walking in the room with her pale, wooden face. And I understood nothing, nothing of how the world was being made all over again around me. As I stood there, every piece was being picked up and scraped off and put somewhere else. I was only a boy walking through the church. The moonlight muffled my footsteps. There was a small door up by the altar. Father Thomas was not there. There was a light burning, and a bowl of soup on his table, but he was not there, because only I was moving! You cannot think there is a Heaven or a Hell, for it is all mixed up together, and that night I was the only one who was moving! There was only a light and the soup.

∞∞

✆ Drinking the Sacred Wine

In the bell tower, I found a bottle of sour red wine that even the soldiers had refused to drink. They were always getting drunk on the steps of the church, and singing badly – but not with this stuff. I grabbed a dusty, cold bottle and ran back into the night. The light off the square burst over me like a wind off the stars. There was the smell of ice on the air. Then I was in the light and I raced across it, and the dark came back up over me like a wing, and I gasped.

I thought, shit, what is this wine like, so I stepped back into a shadow and took a sip. Imagine, getting drunk on church wine! The moon turned a pale, windswept blue. The air was full of the scent of black mud and cow-shit and the cold sea growing thick with fog and woodsmoke. Down a long, muddy row of pollarded poplars, I saw a man walking. He wore a dirty leather jacket, wool trousers, wooden shoes. He came up to me in the lead-grey fog. It was me – returning to the village from the fields – so I turned, and we walked back together. There was a cider orchard beside the road, with a few frozen apples in the branches. The stars were bright in the sky and drifted in long, slow currents with the wind, like flour spilled on a threshing floor, but on one side of the sky it was dark, where they had all blown away. It was a long time ago.

So. That is what it was like.

<hr/>

❦ Unwelcome Visitors

I heard their voices right away, and ducked behind the tall hall table. How little its bevelled glass doors hid *me*! The glass twisted my face completely out of shape. I do not know why they did not see me.

'Shit, Karl. What else is a woman *for!*' They were going into the basement with their flashlights, to see what they could find down there. But then I came home, and I heard them in the basement. They shone their lights crazily on all the walls and on all the shadows, but there was no one there for them to see: the light bounced off the shadows and stuck to the light instead, as if the light were the shadows, where we really were. In the moonlight that night the house was light, and light sticks close to light – it is afraid of the dark and grows brighter the more light is shone on it. Since it does not understand the dark, light does not see the dark.

When Mama came home, the police heard her footsteps and came upstairs immediately, their dogs bounding ahead of them up the stairs, their legs moving like pistons in an engine block. The police choked the dogs back on their leashes, with the clattering of the dogs' nails, and strutted out into the hallway.

Mama hung up her coat and shook the cold and the smoke of the night town from it. The whole town just smelled like a steel foundry, like sulphur. Mama shook it out onto the floor. She saw me there then, through the bevelled glass and crystal of the hall table, my face bent and twisted beside her. She almost said, 'Get out from behind there!' when the police came into the room, laughing to themselves. Mama turned to them without flinching.

'What are you doing in my house?

'Frau Doktor, we were thinking there was trouble here in your house.' The man's voice was greasy.

The other one just coughed.

'Is it the Russian girl?' Mama folded up her gloves, then folded them again, more tightly.

They laughed together. 'That's OK. She's in the kitchen.'

'Crying.'

All pasty and white from that hole of theirs up in Old Town. I watched them through the cut glass.

They followed their dogs out in a big storm of movement. It swirled and coughed, and the house contorted in it, twisted – like mirrors in a show at the circus; a big square box of a house with the iron railings stripped off and dropped on Manchester and the house numbers unscrewed on a foggy morning and melted down in a blast furnace at Bochum and dropped on Southampton – fell right through a house and blew a little baby up into the air, and when she came down she was a pigeon, furiously flapping her wings.

10. The Healing

In those years we were not taught to think. We were taught to feel. In the nightmare of that feeling, thinking was something invisible to us. We made it up. When we thought, we did so with the only thing we could: with our feelings.

My wife, Dorothy, has come back with me to see my town. The house smells of a fir tree, as it has never smelled before. Soon it will be time to go to church, to meet my brothers and sisters. I do not know what they will see – the cold of Canada, or all the cracks and splinters of time collapsing around me, as I sit in the dark of a barn and Death yells in my face and says I am a man, I have done this, I have killed love. I am supposed to love people, but there is no love, only fear. I am supposed to go to church, but all my years in Canada are nothing. Everything I have learned in Canada counts as nothing, because there is no Canada – the fields around town are some country I have never seen before. Everything I went to Canada to run from is waiting for me here and I am too old to hide from it any more. This is who I am. I am the place where the world fights its wars. You cannot make a person out of that. You cannot make a life out of that. We live our lives somewhere where we are invisible, somewhere a long way from ourselves. We live our lives by remote control, as if we are too poisonous to touch.

There is nothing to understand, except we can shape nothing. And we keep on going. It is impossible. The snow is falling softly on the art-nouveau iron railing, and on the peach tree against the garage wall. That is all. This is what I should ask Mama, but I have never asked Mama, because she was there in the barn and said I had to be a man for her, but how was I to do that? Papa was not there. Was I supposed to be the Moroccans, who killed the girl, their officers who killed *them*? Was I supposed to be the police? There was no one. I was on my own. That was what they taught us in those years. That was the purpose of politics: to isolate us. It was meant to hold us to what we could touch and see..That was thinking. And all the time it talked about bringing us together, about uniting us, how the country was our social group. That was totally useless. It made us alone. Now I carry my time within me like a poison. I should have asked Mama what she thought of this, what she saw coming, what she knew, what she knew later, what she made of herself after Blaumann beat her black and blue because she was a woman, because she was a doctor, because she had a self.

<hr/>

✎ A Boar Hunt in the Basement

After the police left, Mama and I found everyone downstairs. Maryushka was bending over Pierre. The light was smoke attempting to be light. Father Thomas was crushing some herbs that Tante Anna had given him. Tante Anna had some hazel sticks. Martha sat on Pierre's bed. Pierre was sitting on a chair at the table as Martha unwrapped the dirty brown bandage from his head. The light poured down on them from our door at the top of the stairs. Their faces lit up brightly on the sides next to us; on the other sides they were dim and brown from their lamp. Their movements blurred. Big dark sooty shadows clung to everything. You could reach down with your finger and wipe them off.

Everything went slowly. Martha unwrapped a bandage and laid it on the table, but Tante Anna saw it there and threw it onto the floor.

'He does not need that.' Her voice was light, almost singing.

Mama stopped at the bottom of the stairs and for a moment stepped no further. 'Hello, Anna,' she said, so slowly, as if underwater. 'Hello, Thomas. Bernd.' She looked puzzled. 'Were the police just here?'

'No,' said Father Thomas.

'They were just upstairs,' Mama said.

Martha kept on unwrapping those bandages!

'Hansel was hiding behind the hallstand. He looked like a fish through the glass. The police were in the kitchen.'

'They did not find us here and we did not see them,' Martha said.

'Not so hard!' whispered Pierre.

I handed Tante the wine. 'They were up there with their dogs. They saw Maryushka crying in the kitchen.'

'Maryushka has been crying in the kitchen all day,' said Martha, slowly. 'What do you expect, then?'

As Mama stepped down off the last stair and into the room, Tante Anna pulled an old handkerchief full of herbs from her pocket. They smelled like the stars. She spilled them into a small wooden bowl.

'Is there anything I can do, Anna?' Mama asked, almost under her breath.

Tante Anna shook her head and poured some of the church wine into the bowl. The wine came out and smelled of rotten grapes. It smelled dead. It smelled of a winter storm. Tante Anna had taken the church, and something so old it had none of the church in it, only trees, and she had mixed it together. It became part of my thinking. One minute it was a watery fall sun, then it was a winter storm, with the first flakes of snow clotting out of the air. The trees shook as men brushed through them, rifles over their shoulders, snapping the fine twigs. The air filled with the scent of the trees. As the boars rushed on ahead, all the children of the town bashed at the bushes, with sticks. The big yellow leaves of the beeches and the brown leaves of the oaks clung to their skin in the damp air, like leeches and scraps of light. As the day died the light sank out of the air and the whole world opened to the stars. The mistletoe clung high up in the oaks, dark, throwing blotty shadows over the thin, wasp shadows of the pines. The boar – mad – burst right out of the bushes; the children ran up the trees – and there was the boar at the bottom, snorting. Tante Anna laid her handkerchief in the bowl, to soak it up.

<hr/>

⚅ Dogs

After she mixed the herbs with the wine, Tante Anna sent the men upstairs. As we walked up, a smell rose past us, above the damp and coal of the basement. I knew the police could smell that too; they could follow it like their dogs, the way some drunk or a priest could follow wine. That is why they always had dogs. They were dogs. They just looked like men! How the dogs had finally managed to do that, who knows! – trying for a long time and everyone knew it, and then one day they had done it! Got right up and walked! And nobody could believe it! Then they believed it alright, because they were mean bastards. What do you expect: people kick dogs. All this time the dogs were trying to get back at them: now they had, and nobody liked it. Ja, everything is changing into everything else. That is what happens in this world. The police liked all that dark leather. They did not even look like people any more! The dogs smell you and know you are afraid.

ooooooooooooooooooooooooooooooooooooooooooooooooooooooooooooooooooooooooooooooooooooooooo

Teeth

Rudi said the police needed a war to get gold for their teeth! It is true, their teeth were completely rotten. You never saw the police biting into apples or potatoes – it hurt them too much. Claus used to pour vodka on his teeth for us children! He filled up his mouth with vodka, swished it around, then swallowed it – and grinned, showing the blackened stumps. We thought the vodka was dissolving his teeth! We thought he was really tough. The police pulled their teeth out all the time, with pliers. Sometimes the teeth broke off. There was no dentist. He was in Russia. They just had to figure it out on their own. Siegfried used to go down there sometimes. He would put on a white apron he got from Max the butcher and go down there and pull their teeth for them with a pair of bent-up, twisted weird pliers he used to use for cow's teeth – when he still had a cow! As he tromped past us on his way down there with that, he would wink at us children. The police would give him something to drink, too. He was the only man who was able to hurt them!

ooooooooooooooooooooooooooooooooooooooooooooooooooooooooooooooooooooooooooooooooooooooooo

The Police

They came from Rastatt, not from our town. When they came, the storks went crazy, restless, never settling in their nests, flying back and forth over the town, down to the swamps of the Old Rhine. Once someone said, 'Hey, it has a snake!' But you could not tell. Whatever it had was all bloody, dangling from that orange scissor beak. It was harder and harder to get to sleep at night. You felt there was somebody in the room with you.

∞∞

❧ The Shoe

Upstairs, Maryushka had all the lights off and the shutters open; staring out into the big houses rising up around us from the dark. It was quiet. The garden that Pierre had clipped and trimmed had vanished into the night. He had showed me the flowers and told me which ones they had in France. Now it was dark and brooding in the thin moon.

All at once the room smelled of wildflowers in the snow; then it smelled like wine that had sat out all night in a glass: sharp, filling the air.

Father Thomas pushed the basement door shut.

'Do you smell anything? I asked.

'Onions,' he snapped.

I pushed my way through the spring door into the kitchen. The door slapped against my palm.

Maryushka looked up. Her eyes were swollen.

'So you had some friends over,' I teased. But I coughed. The smell in the kitchen knocked you right over: onions! Maryushka looked so pathetic. Even today I cannot eat those damn onions. That one terrible day comes on me all at once, when I opened the door to the kitchen after the police had roughed Maryushka up. She looked so pathetic, there at the table, trying to sew her shoes back together with a small, thin needle. Her dress was torn.

'Leave her alone, Hansel,' said Father Thomas, behind me. 'Are you alright? What did they want?'

She said nothing. She tried to push the needle through the thick rubber sole of her shoe.

'Are they coming back?'

'They always come back,' Bernd cut in. 'Each time it gets a little easier. They keep coming until you join them or they kill you. They keep coming for as long as you live.'

Maryushka shoved the needle into the palm of her hand. Blood welled out, red and hot. 'Damn!'

'Bernd!' shouted Father Thomas. 'Can't you do that for her? You are a handworker. Can't you fix her shoes!'

'I make soap. I do not make shoes. I have not made any soap for years. There is no lard.'

He held up his huge, lye-stained fingers. The fingernails were half eaten away. His hands were all brown and blistered.

'Just lye. But I will sew the shoes.' He lifted them gently from Maryushka's hands. With hands like that, it must have hurt him to carry the lard buckets, yet he never complained. 'Thomas, why don't you look at her hand.'

The room flared with the smell of roses. I drank it down, but I felt like a swimmer under stars, swimming for some place far away, deep underwater.

'Pierre,' said Maryushka. 'They came about Pierre.'

'Were they looking for Pierre?' asked Bernd.

'No.' She pulled her hand suddenly away from Father Thomas, who was trying to stop the blood, and wiped it on her apron. 'No. They were just asking.'

'I would have thought that flesh wounds would be your specialty,' said Bernd.

'Maybe your angels could stop it from bleeding,' snapped Father Thomas.

'I doubt it.' Bernd tossed the shoe back to Maryushka. 'You cannot see them except in your dreams. The wind blows them away, or the rain washes them away. They are watching us. They bring us things.'

'I would not want to read any of His messages these days.'

'You are all crazy,' snapped Maryushka. 'There are no angels. There is nothing bringing us anything. There is just God or there is not God. There is nothing more than that!'

'The storks are the angels,' Bernd said. 'With their big white wings flapping above our houses. Don't you think so?'

The room filled with the deep scent of water, so thick it replaced the air in the house.

While Drowning in the Deep Scent of Water

I saw Father Thomas running from the doors of the church into the snow, with the light pouring out behind him, yelling at me, 'Come inside!' I saw Pierre, slipping through the back garden, crossing into the field at the end of the block, where there were no more houses. It was black, with stars – like fish at the bottom of the river, eels moving in and out of the trees. Ditch by ditch, slowly under scattered, wind-shattered stars, he made his way to the river, the light catching at his hair, sinking into it. I caught it in scraps, as if the wind were shredding the message as it brought it to me: a stupid wind, dropping pieces of it, picking them up again, denting them, and getting them in the wrong order. There was light in his hair. The wind tossed it over his face.

The House Disappears

There was the sound of laughter from downstairs again – my sister's, loud, and Tante Anna's like sticks scraped together – then the smell flowed just as suddenly out of the air, and there was only the smell of onions. Maryushka cried out, 'The bleeding has stopped!'

We stared at her.

'You had better go downstairs with the other women. They are going to need you,' said Bernd, breaking the silence.

As Maryushka opened the basement door the smell of dampness and flowers and trees blew up – a whole forest was growing down there, a mountain wind, the trees swaying, their branches heavy with snow. The whole house swam with it, and then disappeared.

11. Return

Every time we remember, we remember a different world, but in all of them I ring the bell and then run back through the wet, sloppy rain. The rain was soaking my shirt, plastering it to my back, heavy and warm as I ran up the steps and pushed open the door with my hands then shook the rain out of my hair. Mama was still at the hospital. The only light was in the kitchen, that high, white room with one window looking out on the back garden and the night.

Maryushka looked up startled from the sink, where she was washing her hands for dinner. In the instant and fear of that look, I saw a huge bird staring in the window – a giant stork made of straw! Then it was burning. The light flapped and clattered in the room, over everything; everything was on fire. Mama came in, waltzing. She picked up onion peels and threw them at the window. The fire went out. Those little onion peels broke the window! I looked out. There was no night and no stars. The air was one vast star that had swallowed us. Then the blind was back on the window. The electric light seemed pale, made of burning oil, as yellow and thin as candlelight. I stood in the doorway, out of breath.

You only see the world in memory, but when you see it, it is a dream. Maryushka quickly dried her hands on her apron and wiped the tears from her eyes with her knuckles. She picked up a plate and hurried into the dining room with dinner: three onions, washed and peeled. She set them on the plates, with her back to me, starched and tense, but her tears did not stop.

There was a lot to understand, because I had been there before like that, I had always been there in the white heart of the house. I had stood there before in the doorway, my shirt clinging to my back with rain, watching Maryushka sobbing over the sink, her face puffy. I knew I had been there before, and before and before; I had always stood there, so it must have been my entrance into the room that teased her – over and over and over she had to be there for me, crying over the sink. She must have seen in me all that backward time, the way you lean over the edge of a cliff and drop a rock and watch it fall. It was as if I knew that moment so well she could not surprise me with it. There was shock in her eyes, but not on her face: her face was crying. Far back in her eyes, like fish passing quickly in deep water, I knew I had been there before in that moment – she was living it for the first time! Suddenly you see the darkness of your body. I was trying to figure it out, trying to decipher if somehow the world had bent so badly around us that I was returning again and again to one time, or whether we were all going back to one minute of fear. You are awkward, for you have just discovered how easily you can touch your body, or hurt it! Maryushka looked at me as if there were a hundred of me standing before her, breaking up back into time, each dressed differently. I followed her into the kitchen.

'Pierre left last night,' she said.

'He could hardly walk!'

'He could walk well.'

She broke into tears again. We saw the whole moment around us, a thousand times. We knew what was going to happen. We waited. When they came, one of the police came to the back door, one to the front. They came right in on us, first the one from the back door and then, his footsteps louder with every step down the hall, the other; with those dry leather boots, with their sharp faces and their rotten teeth.

As we knew they would, they started to poke through the cupboards, a thousand times, broken up all around us, banging them open and shut. They did not get them all shut. They would bang their heads into them then smash them shut even harder, and the cupboards would burst back open as if they were too full to shut. One of the police picked up a glass of water from the table, took a deep drink of it, like a horse! He spat it all back up again, spraying it in Maryushka's face.

'It tastes like piss!'

A thousand beefy-faced men around us did the same.

Maryushka did not answer. It was silent. 'We are looking here,' the other one said, 'and in all the houses in this part of town. Someone has been looking after a Frenchman. We thought, "So, go see the Frau Doktor. If he is shot up, she will know!" They laughed, then turned out of the kitchen and stomped down the stairs to the basement, in their heavy black boots. As soon as they did, all the thousand facets of time disappeared. We were alone in a cold, dim room. The moonlight skittered under the door like snow. I sat there with Maryushka, scared.

<hr />

❀ Nobody

Maybe there was more than one kind of angel, I thought. There could be all kinds, depending on what questions God needed to ask, or what messages he wanted to send. The police, with their eyes like flat blue stones, their pimply faces and bad breath, were some kind of a message in a time that is solid, that you can move through.

This life has a thousand doors. You see them in your dreams. The floorboards are worn down to splinters. You open one door and see a river, and a coal barge out on the river; open another door: a man is cooking turnip soup, but he is using his own hand as the soup bone! He has his whole arm in the soup, stirring it. You close that door and walk and walk. Through another door, it is a fat man, laughing very loudly. Through another door you see snow. In the snow, there is something dark. Someone is standing there – he starts to struggle through the snow to get to you. You are not sure – it might be a tree. You shiver, and close the door. Through another door you see a boy who looks like you, but he is made of wax. There is a wick in the top of his head and it is burning with a little flame. A hot dribble of black wax runs down his face. You close the door.

I never went through any of the doors. I could not do it. I was still looking for God. So, what is gonna make me get through, I wondered. God, maybe – kick you in the ass with boots made of thistles. Or he is a big Belgian workhorse, with long, muddy hair over his hooves. He is tired, from dragging a stupid plough through the field all day, down one side of the field and back up the other side in the clay, and stupid leather harnesses and rings, so tired, and you get too close and he gives you a big kick, pow – and there you are, flying into the door. You land inside on your face, the door right under you. It could be any bloody damn thing, but I do not know because I never got through the door and I do not know what could get you through the door.

It was as if everyone else had passed through the doors and growing always more frantic, I could not: they had filled all the rooms and there was not one for me. I kept opening the doors, thinking this is an empty one, but there never was. As if everyone had passed through the doors – and I was frantic, and I could not.

12. The Cold Attic Room

⊛ Fear

Mama told me. 'You cannot beat the enemy by being afraid. When a man has lost his arms and legs, when his whole face is burned or his lungs are scorched and he breathes as if he is breathing through the sole of a shoe, death comes. Death is weak. In this war you cannot tell who the enemy is: you see death everywhere; everyone lives for it; it seems stronger than anything, but it is not. It does not meet you face to face. It is persistent, ja. It keeps knocking at the door, and the sound shakes through the whole house and through your dreams until you feel strong in yourself and sick of all the noise, the hammering and kicking at the door, and sick of the silence when it sleeps curled up on the step outside. One day you get so annoyed at the noise and the silence after it that you open the door to tell death to leave you alone, but there is absolutely nothing there, not even the thought of nothing! Then death has you. That is where the police have gone. We opened the door and came down and they were not there. As long as we had the door closed they were there and we were not. In its weakness death is strong.

'The third time we washed Pierre, his wounds healed. We sent him off through the garden. The police brought him into the hospital, with their muddy boots all over my floor. A patrol scared him up by the river. He was dead. You do not cheat death. It has all the time in the world! You can hold it back a little, that is all. So, we got him out of the house. He is gone from here, so the police did not find him here. Time will do that. It will slither away and bite its tail with its mouth.'

⊛ A New Message, a New Messenger

The fear was breathing slowly along with me, breath by breath, 'Do you think there are angels?'

Mama laughed and pressed me close to her, deep into her breasts, almost smothering me in her smell. 'No, Hansel. There is life and there is death, but there are no angels.'

How could God get his message to us without angels? With no messengers there was no message! It was not that God could do anything or everything – if we could not hear, he could not get the message to us.

∞∞∞

◎ The Sulphurous Taste of Onions

Maryushka was crying, but now she was laughing with it. Mama put her arm around Maryushka and led her into the dining room and had her sit with us. That night Mama burned one of the candles she had been saving for Christmas, in the candelabra with the three arms and the milky colours of the silver. You would think someone spent all day polishing it, but it just came out of the cupboard!

In the dim, flickering light of that one candle, we ate: onions; one set on each of the four plates, washed and peeled. I was sick at the smell. They smelled of the rain when Pierre and I had picked off the slugs that were eating them in the garden. I pushed my plate over to my skinny sister and went upstairs into the cool of my attic. As I walked up the stairs I could hear Martha's knife clinking on the plate.

I cannot stand it even now. Every piece of this memory is onion.

∞∞∞

◎ The Iron Sky

I heard the storks walking on the roof, scraping over the tiles like the wind with his dull iron axe and his bundle of sticks, trying to get down the chimney. Even in the attic it smelled like the coke in the back yard! It was as black as coal dust, with the storks walking over the roof above me like miners digging underground. Open to the wind, on the edge of town, the attic sounded like the whole sky was scraping tile by tile over the roof – a steel sky. With the smell of dust from the basement on my fingers I lay in bed as if there was only my hunger there, until there was nothing there, only hunger,

shredding and drawn away in the wind until I was only the smell of
the wind, then only the wind.

❦ The Millstone: Franzel Said

'It is from the Swedes. When they surrounded our town, they carried that stupid millstone with them. It is very heavy. When they
cleared out in such a hurry they did not take it back! Instead, they
hurled it into town on a catapult: a joke, ja – so we could grind our
bread with it, just to make us hungrier. It landed in the middle of
the square and bust up the blue and gold statue of Mary that used
to stand there. Father Thomas has the pieces in a back corner in
the church basement – she was smashed. The millstone was
unbroken. The men dragged it up to the barn. It is still there. I still
grind my grain on it.'

The flour ground on that stone was tough and gritty, but it
tasted like the wheat out in the windy fields, like a whole long day
of sun.

I helped Franzel there, but that was a long time ago, you do
what you have to do. It is so long ago it is a different country.
Those pieces of the Virgin made seeds sprout in the dead of the
winter. Onions shrivelled right up. Father Thomas spread his
onions out there once, down by the furnace, to dry them. They all
went black!

❦ Whom Do I Speak to in the Night, in What Time of the World?

We whisper messages and warnings to ourselves while we sleep,
when we see into time, but when we wake, and can actually act on
it, we do not hear. It tears us apart. We are all two people.

⊛ Angels in the Attic

The morning light was white and pale over the walls. The walls were cracked, right above my bed. They had buckled inwards. My back hurt from being twisted under the eiderdown all night. Since the start of the war the eiderdown had grown too small. I had to twist myself to make myself fit under it. I lay there, only half-awake. The whole world was shrinking. The light lay over everything, every little crack and ripple, without a shadow.

When I opened my eyes again, my two worlds had come together. The war was close. There was a big crowd at the foot of the bed. There were two tall angels dressed in shiny gold, with red flaming hair and pale lips, looking bored and scratching at their scales with their claws, unblinking. They just watched. I looked around: there were angels all around the room. When I blinked and opened my eyes again, they were gone. The stillness had soaked into the walls.

I threw the covers off. The wind had stopped. The light and the house were still. I listened, but I heard none of the sound of the town: not the police dogs, not the sound of Bernd's lard pails banging against each other, not Maria throwing open the shutters on her bedroom window or Frau Kapp beating her rug and coughing out the dust. It was as if the world had ceased to exist. I pushed myself from bed into the silence. For a second I thought I heard the angels scratching themselves, pulling back the covers and crawling in to sleep, thumping the pillow with their hands, and the window being pushed open. But there was nothing. My body shuddered once, with cold, then slowly walked downstairs.

The house was empty. The echo of the house and the real house were nowhere around. The house was rushing through the air, tossing and turning – a balloon when you let the air out of it.

The years were not there.

Maryushka had gone out to the market to look for something to eat. There was nothing to buy. Mama had already left for the hospital.

These days silence is full of creaking and footsteps and voices a long way away. You can almost catch what they are saying, rippled and turned into air by the way they have gone through air – wind full of the sounds of trees creaking, breaking themselves apart; water turning to ice in the mouth. In those days it was something all by itself. That morning it was a house and it was silence – two things filling the same space at the same time, shadows of shadows. You could not turn your thinking away from one to see the other. You could only walk through them. You could not think at all. You could only be the points things passed through. I poured myself a glass of water and drank it down, then another glass. Outside there was still no sound. High above, clouds were black and boiling in the air. A slow cold wind was sinking from them, the whole sky slowly draining into the earth. The streets were covered with clots of straw and small clumps of manure, and pools of brown water. My footsteps were soundless. I was walking through a heavy fog, but there was no fog, no sound at all until I reached the square. I was walking deep back down through my memory. Something was waiting for me, a terrible animal ready to swallow me. I had to face it. I stepped into the square. There the army trucks were passing, roaring through, the sound echoing off the close walls. The diesel fumes filled the air between the houses, churned up by trucks going by and the flapping of the canvas, but they did not get pushed up into Old Town, they just grew thicker and thicker right where they were.

◈ In the Roar of Trucks

It was as if the trucks had driven straight out of the air and were driving straight back into it on the other side of town! Time was all bent and twisted. It had taken a direct hit! The girders of time were just a heap of twisted metal; you never knew what was going to happen next. Shit, there must have been some action down at the river.

For hours and hours the trucks passed through town. Everywhere people went in Old Town that sound followed them, twisting around corners, fading out. Suddenly they would bang into it again as they came around another corner. It had found a different path, an easier way up through the houses! Like water, it spread out in ripples, slowly, up through the narrow, twisted streets and filled them.

When the big offensive came along the river the bunkers and all the fields around were blown all to shit and there were more army trucks than ever before, all through the night, tanks too, splintering the cobbles. No one in town slept. Our dreams sat with us on our beds, or took turns with us staring out our windows as the stars fell out of the air and started to burn away the fields, fizzling in the damp grass.

Once a wolf paced in the room. He stood in the half dark just past the edge of the moonlight. He never stepped out into the clear light.

You do not doubt yourself. You forget yourself altogether.

When we got up in the morning the trucks would be gone, but all the houses would still be shaking with their passage. A thin eggshell light flooded between the fields and the clouds. When the sun came through, everything was terribly still, as if it had been washed. We stood in the doorways, and a bit of wind – just little scraps of wind – scurried around our feet, like a little dog.

@ Walking Uphill

I dashed through a gap between two trucks. The driver had to slam on his brakes. He yelled at me through his open window, but I was already past, in the ripples of dust the trucks were throwing out on the far side of the street. All the houses were grey. The air was thick. When I looked back down through the twisted streets, way down at the end like a little knot in a rope, through the hazy gases of the trucks, was Father Thomas's church, small and tired. Through that tiny crack between it and the house facing it, truck after truck passed by, just a flash in low gear, roaring, truck after truck after truck, all the way up through Old Town. The storks rose and settled on their rooftops, scattering, white as scraps of washing.

In Old Town the sky was closer, and stronger. It had the smell of the basement of an old church; damp.

If Mama was not dead now, she would say, 'That is why I never chose to live in the old town, Hansel!'

That morning the air smelled of snow, swirling in. I hurried on to Rudi's.

∞∞∞

◎ The Barns: Franzel

'They built those old houses with the barns underneath. As they were putting the houses up, all the cows walked among the stones. Then it started to snow. The people thought they would be unable to finish before the cold set in. That night, they tried to build the walls in the dark, but their fingers were frozen. Then people walked out of the snow and started helping. The barns were built in one night, in torchlight, in the snow! That was the worst winter ever. Huge flakes of snow came down like pieces of the moon. The doors were hung as dawn began to fill the air, glowing about them – the sun had come down from the sky and was burning around them in the snow! All the people of the night were gone. They had built the barn. The cows! Ja, Hansel, when the cows were brought into the barns in the morning they remembered every rock, the way they had lain out in the fields, and went up to each rock and nudged it with their cold, wet noses. The cows! They had come in the snow but in the light they were gone, as if they were formed from snow, swirling as it blows in the air. Then it can come alive. That is why I am not leaving this house – not ever.'

13. Air Attack

⚙ Shovelling

Rudi was shovelling. He was up to his knees.

'Rudi!' I called into the dark of the barn. The ammonia burned from the door, with the hay smell riding over it like a violin, la, la, la, la, la. Rudi was shovelling the manure out the open doorway into Franzel's big wooden cart that stood in front of it.

'Hello, Hans. This is for dinner.'

Like nearly all the boys, I did small jobs for Franzel. Then she would feed us: eggs, cheese, bread and milk. Turnips too! I would go out with her on the wagon and sit up front with her, with the hay creaking behind us. We would plant the spuds and then at night I would go out on those wet black lanes into the fields and dig them up again, to eat them!

So I helped Rudi. I stomped the shovel around the feet of the cows. I started scraping the shit out and then got right down to the floorboards underneath, curling up a thin shaving of the wet, soaking wood with the tip of the shovel. Rudi dug beside me, and soon, under that low dark ceiling – burned by a fire many years before – we had the barn cleaned out.

I sat on the milking stool in the dairy room and washed my shoes in a bucket. The cows flicked their tails beside me, their huge bony sides steaming with warmth, while Rudi got his food from Franzel. When he returned, he had a piece of greasy sausage sticking from his mouth. He bit off a piece, and threw me the rest. We sat for a minute, the manure ground down under our fingernails, and ate the sausage, coughing, fast. Then we stepped outside into the blowing sunlight. The roar from the trucks broke over us. We walked up through it to Rudi's, squinting against the sudden light. Everything was white and glaring in our eyes. Something was changing. Something was blowing away.

Ten minutes later we were riding Rudi's new bike out of town, wobbling on that dusty back road to Rastatt. I sat on the handlebars, with my feet resting on the bolts for the axle. Rudi puffed and pedalled us both along.

Rastatt was bigger than our town. It was an industrial centre, with train yards and factories. Its long streets of factories and engine works had been blown up into piles of broken bricks, potholes filled with the yellow soup that trickled out of the ashes, and big twisted beams of fire-blackened metal. Most of the beams had been cut away and trucked off to make shell casings, but there were still big chunks of them jutting from the ruins, the metal black and bubbly where it had been cut by gas torches, there where nothing grows, where everything was brown and black, and the wind blew hollowly over the cut ends of water pipes. A huge black crow scattered up in front of us from one of the puddles. Its reflection was completely yellow – a yellow crow right there! We wobbled in on the bicycle, then we slid sideways and tumbled together into the puddle.

I came up spluttering. The dirty yellow water was in my clothes and running down my face. It tasted chalky and awful. I spat it out and wiped my tongue on my sleeve, but I could not get the taste out. I swore at Rudi about his riding, and he swore at me about being so heavy! Heavy! I had not eaten for days. I hardly weighed a thing! So he could not blame it on me!

We hung our clothes over a crumbling brick wall. It was in the early morning and the sun was weak. Clumps of grass were sprouting from the bottom of the bricks, and we sat there with the wind shivering over our pale, thin chests. I picked the manure from my fingernails. The clouds were white and blew overhead like a dream. It seemed as if there was nothing in the world that could hurt us, but one of those clouds passed in front of the sun for a minute and it was cold in the shadow, as cold as the water that lies right on the bed of the river, passed over by the current. For a second I was really cold.

As the shadow sank over the buildings around us I saw the buildings suddenly as they were years before, when I first saw them at the beginning of the war. In the howling of the air-raid alarms the noise had screamed and split the air. Every piece of the air had split apart from every other piece. Rudi and I had jumped off the stupid, slow school-train and had walked up to the industrial section where the bombing had gone on the day before, right where we were sitting years later, drying our clothes, with the wind running its hand over our chests. In the shadows of the clouds I saw it all again: the brick and glass scattered over the streets, trucks smashed on their sides and still smoking with green, rotting smoke, and a few yellow fires still burning – brilliant flames rising over the big factories: Daimler Benz, BMW, Siemens. I saw the signs burning, the smoke drifting with the wind, and the new bomb craters in the street full of air without any edges – it was all the air in the world.

The shadow was growing darker. It was all growing stronger – like a photograph developing right before our eyes.

I said to Rudi, 'Come on! Something's going to happen!'

I did not need to say it, because he could tell too.

Then I saw the plane, a small silver flash down by the railyards where all our schoolfriends, our whole second-grade class, were killed in those days of radios at the start of this war that had replaced the world. I saw it there, bobbing through the air, the sunlight catching again and again at its wings as I struggled back into my wet clothes. All the time the smell of lime rose in my nostrils. That American plane was down there, shooting the ruins of the station, with the track twisted up. I did not see him: I saw those planes come those three years before, and I saw their bombs fall. The planes filled the sky. They were silver, there and there and there. They dropped their bombs on the station.

They were beautiful when they fell, fluttering, and of course terrible, and blew the station all to bits. The smoke towered up as high as the planes. I saw a pit and in that hole all my friends, and workers throwing lime on them to eat them away, shovelfuls of it. Flash! Flash! Oh, shit. Then Rudi was on the bicycle, riding away. I was running beside him, through that maze of twisted, empty streets. I saw in each puddle another piece of the past: Rudi's face as he looked down with me into that hole full of all our friends; the face of a young girl, little Babs, her hair burnt away and yet her dress, goddamn it, clean and still pressed, with hardly even a stain on it, a frilly dress, like a party dress, with polka dots and shit, lace and stuff. I saw the big windows of the factories shattered into long knives of glass, and how the glass was, each piece scattered in chips and slivers over the street, reflecting the sky, as if the sky was shattered, scattered all over the street, every piece burning with a different sort of sky – blue sky without clouds, and grey sky like rotten grass; rain streaming down; slow floating snow; clouds shredding in storm; colourful sunsets with small specks of birds; dark sky with smoking stars. We were in the sky. There was no ground under our feet, only glass. Some of the pools I splashed through were huge pools of fire! As the water sprayed around me, there was fire on my pants, and splashes of fire on my face and hands. Some of the pools seemed to be smoke, grey smoke or yellow smoke, boiling, and thin threads of smoke, poison. I ran on beside Rudi. My breath was bursting as he rode crazily around the puddles, trying not to get any of the dirty water on himself. Ja, Rudi, he did that, of all crazy things to do at a time like that! He was always like that. He could just crack you up! Ja, because it would stain his bike and ruin it! His new bike!

Suddenly we turned a corner. The plane was there. He was no longer down at the station. I could see the pilot. He was one of these American niggers, in a Lightning. He had a smile on his face as he came for us! Suddenly the bullets were spitting down. Rudi dropped his bike and jumped into an old boiler that was there in the loading yard behind an old factory. There was room only for Rudi – it was not a large boiler, it did not have all that much room! I dove onto the ground behind it, down in the greasy lemon-smell, the gravel behind the concrete footings, on the rusted iron. I had just thrown myself down there when the plane passed again, spraying the boiler with bullets. That old boiler hollered and shouted – like you had jammed your head into a church bell! The plane turned – the pilot saw me, my face rubbed into the gravel; he turned – he was out to kill us! I scrambled up in that racket, and threw myself down on the other side of the boiler, in the greasy gravel. I wanted to run, but there was no time! He shot at the boiler, and Rudi screamed with the noise, and I yelled at Rudi to see if he was alright, and he just kept on screaming.

The American played with us for half an hour like that, first coming from one side of the boiler, then from the other, just playing with us, just whiling away a bit of his time on us until he ran out of bullets or was running low on gas, God I do not know, I do not have any idea, I do not know why he did it, but he did it. He hunted us like a cat hunts a mouse.

❦ Rats

Everyone's house just stank of rats. I do not know what they ate. There was nothing for anybody to eat, yet there were all these rats – long, black, greasy rats with tails like pieces of rope. They were even up there by the boiler, and when that American started shooting us they ran out screaming and scattered in all directions. The plane came back and I had my face buried in the gravel again, eating the dirt, and the damn boiler clanging and ringing with the bullets. All the time I was thinking about the black and piss-dark time Rudi and I were bombed out in Rastatt – two days in a musty, stinking basement, without any air, under the fires. So there was part of me, a part of me grew more and more calm the longer the strafing went on, so it was ready for the silence that came when the plane had left.

∞∞∞

❦ Turning to Stone

There must have been more than a hundred bullet holes in that rusty old boiler. Rudi was crying on the bottom, his face pressed into a litter of rust flakes and old chemical sludge – a real yellow stuff like egg yolks. Every bullet that hit the boiler had knocked more and more flakes of rust on him, and clouds of rust, fine stuff into the air so he could hardly breathe.

After the plane left, the sound of the boiler ringing with gunfire died out slowly. Every shot rang out, over and under every other shot, and only slowly did they die out, like a fucking church bell. Then it was silent, like when you pound a nail into a wall, crack the plaster, then hang a picture on the nail, or when you stick a key into a lock, or when a cat stares at the corner of a door for it to open. Damn, it all came back to me as I was eating gravel there, dodging those bullets, as the plane came from one side and then banked over the broken-up buildings behind me and I threw myself up and dove into the gravel on the other side of the boiler, over and over.

All the while the moon sat on the top of the boiler like a ghost, telling me over and over to turn into a stone. Turn into a stone!

Turn into a stone! Turn into a stone! Turn into a stone! Turn into a stone! Over and over and over. Telling me that. Sitting up on the boiler like a stork. The gravel would spit up around me with the bullets, and I lay there, eating gravel.

I saw the sun walk up to me and lie down with me so that my clothes started to burn and when I raised my arms the flames were feathers and I floated up. When the plane came again I could look the pilot right in the eye! But he did not look back. I was cold. Ja, it all came back to me, I was there. In Rastatt.

We had gone in that day on the train to see Rudi's grandma. Rudi figured she would have something to eat! He was right too.

It was so silent. It was all so slow. I knew then: that nigger in the plane, who looked me in the eye, was God. Why he flew away again, I do not know! I told him to go away and then he did, and I do not understand it. One minute he wanted to kill us; the next minute he wanted to leave. My mind went quiet with it. I had chased God away. It was my fault! But what was I supposed to do: he was trying to kill me! I was just a boy – how could I be responsible for that, how could I bear that? Shit, I saw Rudi's grandmother standing in a puddle right in front of me, in an open place of weeds and bricks and shit just past the boiler. Ja. In a stupid old flowered dress. With a dirty white apron. I took a deep breath and she was not there.

∞∞∞

Dresden China in the Middle of the Street

Grandmothers always had something for you to eat, but it was cooked badly – or overcooked. They had forgotten how to cook properly long ago. The cakes were raw in the middle and burnt to the bottom of the pan. The peas were as dry as flour. The carrots were bitter and soft.

Rudi's grandma lived in a small apartment high up on Wasserengelstraße in Rastatt – high, angry-looking buildings where the plane trees were pruned hard, their bark peeling off in big scabby green and brown chunks, pruned back to three or four small twigs to draw the sap – to draw the sap! She must not have aired the place out for years! That air must have been there in that room since the last war, with its smell of lavender and its old woman stink. Everything in the room, the dried strawflowers on the side table, dusty and crisp as tissue paper, the papery skin that crinkled on her cheekbones, everything was drying up and withering away. We sat on the hard, high-backed couch. Her fingers shook. She was pouring each of us a little peppermint tea. She had old Dresden china – very thin, as clear as onion skins – with little angels all the way around the gold rim, chubby little guys with trumpets, on a silver tray as black as coal dust. She was old. She gave us each òne piece of cake. It was some sort of horse-oats and plum cake she had made. She had not made it for us – she did not know we were coming. She did not have sugar, so it was very sour. There was a plum tree in the back garden, a small tree with cankers and hard green plums – a seedling tree, where someone had spat a pit. It had grown there in the back of the garden, and gave sour plums that no one else wanted – and she made a cake.

We sat in that stale air choking back that cake. Sometimes we would hear someone call out somewhere else in the building: laughing, people going up and down the stairs – hollow sounds. When she offered us another piece we took it. We washed it down with her weak, dusty, mint tea. The mint smell floated out of the thin china cups like summer, but the mint had almost no taste. Then the sirens went off and I spilled the tea. The American planes were coming! A guard pounded at the door and said, 'Everyone go down to the basement!' – where we could be safe.

Rudi's grandma said, 'I am not going down. I am not leaving my place. You do not win a war by running away!' But we could hear the bombs. Maybe half a kilometre away!

Rudi and I pleaded with the stupid old woman. Shit, the bombs were coming closer! They moved closer and closer, like a wall moving down all the streets. The houses around us started to blow up, but the stupid old woman was so attached to her things – all the rubbish of her life, china and flowers, that she did not care any more about her life!

We just could not understand. After a long life they are the same thing. You do not leave things again, all the shit we carry around with us, that is what memory is, it is no damn good. You need all those other things to remember for you, and you get scared when you get old – you do not trust anything any more. We just thought she was a stupid old woman.

The bombs were falling down the street. You had to wait for it, for them to come? Christ. The building started to shake with the farthest explosions. That was not so far away really! We got her down into the basement – just in time, because a huge bastard landed right on top of the building and levelled it. The basement shook around us and pieces of the roof fell in. Then the air filled with dust. There we were, in the dark, in the basement of her building. We could not get out and we could not see.

Slowly I saw people there, but all covered in dust. They were not the same people who were there when the house was hit! They were not the same people! You bang up a house like that and every-thing gets shuffled. They were the worst two days of my life. If you had to piss or shit, you just had to do it in a corner. Everyone did it in the corner, and we all had to smell it down there.

There was a little to eat, but not much. You sure learned what were good people and what were bad. Some gave you their piece of bread, because we were children. Others, grown people, tried to snatch it from us. Some people tried to calm us all, telling stories.

⬢ The Black Cats of Rastatt

Ja, there was a fountain in the middle of Rastatt. When the Swedes came into town they would not let anyone else use it. When people in the town came for water, the Swedes sent them away. It was very hot those days. For water, the people had to go all the way to the Rhine. The Swedes liked to waste their time like that! The people spent most of their time getting water! They started getting angry – because if they spent all that time getting water they did not have any time to go out farming.

One night around that time the cats showed up. They could see in the dark and walked through the night streets, slipping down off the walls. The Swedes did not try to chase them away. That was the people. They were so angry about the water and so tired from going all that dusty hot way to the Rhine that their dreams started to walk around in the town – these cats! They were all colours, but the biggest of them were black. They went up to the fountain and got water when they needed it, when they wanted it, just lapped it up. The hot summer wind blew over town and the grasshoppers ate the fields, burst in clouds in front of you whenever you went out through the grass. The people had more time to go out farming, and that saved them, in that hard winter, when the Swedes left!

You could still smell the cat stink down there in that basement, in Rastatt. You get that into something it never comes out.

That fountain in town, that the Swedes would not let anyone drink from – that is what they thought! – stopped running with water. In the daytime, it ran with wine! The Swedes got drunk. They made a lot of trouble. They were not supposed to drink, but they just guzzled out of that fountain. As soon as the Swedes left, the fountain ran with water again, cool, clear mountain water. That made the people mad!

∞∞

ⓐ Blind to the World

Some people, grown people, just cried and screamed until someone yelled at them, 'Shut up!' then whimpered until someone else slapped them across the mouth. Then they were quiet. We were in the basement for two days and two nights, until the firemen dug us out. You could not tell if it was day or night. You were trapped in your own thinking. You did not dream down there, or you did not wake, it was all the same thing.

People are just terrible. People just make you sick. I was eight years old. Down there, I told myself, 'If people go one way, I will go some other way. I will run out into the street. I will hide somewhere. I will not go in a basement.' I did not tell anyone. I just kept that promise. I had to run from the guards, but it was the most important thing I ever did. The firemen dug us out through the side of the basement into the garden! The plum tree was snapped off. Why they did not use the escape door that had been built right in the middle of the basement, I do not know.

When we stumbled out into the light, I could not see. I saw only lights, and blurry shapes. Slowly they steadied into people. There was Michel. He had come to take us home. Rudi's grandma came back to our town. All her china was broken up. The air had all been blown out of her room. Her whole apartment had been blown to dust and broken bricks. There was glass all over the street and bits of china. There was one little Dresden figure. I picked it up. It was not broken at all. It was a little girl dipping water out of a well. There was a frog! I put it in my pocket. It felt smooth in my hand, and cool. When the bomb fell, something in Rudi's grandma was blown up too, like an over-ripe puffball; you step on it – poof! Ja, like china dropping fifty metres into a street, smashing on the bricks.

ooooooooooooooooooooooooooooooooooooooooooooooooooooooooooooooooooooooooooooooooooooooooooooooo

@ A Slow Bell

Time went slower and slower by the boiler and I could see the bullets passing me in the air like small birds. I could shift to make way for them, and the stars sang overhead – like hymns in a church! It went slower and slower until when there was silence at last I lay perfectly still for five minutes. For five minutes the stars flickered through the blue air like candles in a little girl's hand. I could not tell if I was still being shot at; I was still waiting for the next bullet. Only when the ringing of the boiler died out on the air and Rudi climbed out did I lift my head. The poor guy was half deaf from the explosions of the bullets splashing against the steel. What I saw was just the blue sky and white clouds, and there was Rudi, brushing the rust out of his hair, his face smeared with some powdery yellow chemical. At first he did not hear me at all, then slowly his hearing came back. He said, 'I can hear, but there is this ringing!' He could hear that boiler ringing for weeks, a slow bell tolling on the thinnest part of the air. I could not get out of my head the hate in the pilot's eyes. Rudi's new bike was blown all to hell. It was just a twisted pile of metal, so we left it there with all the busted-up shit. We no longer felt like going anywhere that day; we just walked home. We got home at dusk. It was a long trip, and ever since then I have heard the footsteps of the angels in my dreams, walking away, echoing.

14. The Trip Home

As we made our way home on the dusty back roads through the
alder and hawthorn hedges which lined the pastures, Rudi moaned,
'I feel sick. All that shit in the boiler.'

He looked sick. His skin was in a terrible rash. His breath was
harsh in his throat, thick and scraping out.

The light was low. We broke across the empty fields and long,
long shadows. A few frightened birds called in warning from tree to
tree – crows, scattering up and settling like sad dreams. My nerves
were gone. Rudi, with his golden face, choking on his own breath,
smelled like bleach. We broke through sharp thorn trees, stumbling from field to field. Shadows slipped through the hedges like
bundles of snakes, clutching close to each other to keep warm.
Rudi was so sick, throwing up. It was so far to get back home,
while the sun burned through the sky above us, huge, as if someone had pumped it full and it was filling half the sky – bloated.

There was no time for talk. We were nearing the river. We heard
it first – a slow wind. We knew the army was walking around
somewhere in those fields that flooded every spring, where the
drainage ditches had all grown over so long before.

I heard the planes come, high up. They came every day. We
watched them, flickering between the clouds, catching the high,
cold sun. We did not hear it – it was just a shaking inside us, and we
knew it was there. The bells began to ring out from our church,
long and clear on the air, thin at that distance, then from all the
other villages on the higher ground against the forest. The
churches on the lower ground had all been blown to hell long
before. They were all ruins, piles of bricks – maybe the bell tower
was broken off and the whole doorway underneath was piled with
bricks. The bells echoed and called to each other from all the villages and up to the smoky clouds, a great whining cry to God, or
children burning a straw man, maybe the Father – hanging him
from a tree branch in his old clothes! It was a cry like a woman
with her newborn baby dead in her arms. All the dogs barked in the
villages in the lowlands and the muddy fields, barking and calling
and answering to each other, and the bells over it all, and over
them all the clear bell of our town. The sound of the bells died

away and the dark began to pool and thicken in the air. The clouds froze, then it was dark as a thought trapped inside what you wanted to say, the night that was the night when the night was not there.

∞∞∞

❖ The Bunker

Two months earlier, my youth group had come to those same fields. I saw searchlights then, sudden, sweeping through the sky, carving up big black chunks of the night so they drifted loose. In those hot, sweaty days we dropped down rough-welded iron ladders into a bunker set deep in the sand back from the Rhine. We were scared shitless – we did not know what waited for us down there, only that we had become men. The bunker was filled with rough, broken soldiers sent there to rest. We learned about women too – what they are for, how to use them. We were down from our camp for glider training. The soldiers were proud to show us how they lived. When we came down the metal ladders, the soldiers started to suck their thumbs – and gave us candy, in those concrete tombholes. They showed it all to us – the gun placements, the guard posts, the kitchens, and the deep rooms, with their train lines, where the shells were. And the sappers showed us the dynamite they had wired to the bridge across the river.

∞∞∞

❖ The Moving Silence

Rudi and I were slowly scrabbling through the dark hedges and the low, muddy fields. The sound of the river grew louder until it filled the air, each pebble turning against each other pebble, echoing through the water. We heard the eels slip through the sound, feeding on the water itself.

When we stumbled into town, its shadows swallowed us. We did not know it, but the silence was on the move – moving out in the darkness, to trap the army.

It took us the night. When I awoke, I was lying in bed, in my cold, unheated attic room, with the first snow drifting in around the corners of the glass and making me shiver. I could hear Maryushka laughing downstairs. I went down, and I did not know how I got there – home – out of the fields.

ooooooooooooooooooooooooooooooooooooooooooooooooooooooooooooooooooooooooooooooooooooooooooooooooooo

Home

I come downstairs from Dorothy and that heatless attic room. A cold draft is blowing through the house; voices: Maryushka's, and men's, but when I push open the swinging door to the kitchen, there is nothing there, only echoes in an empty room. Just what you are doing right now can stick out into the past.

I run my fingers over the paint on the edge of the door and I feel it all: those terrible sleepless nights of the plane coming for me, after I had married in Canada, so far away. Canada was where that plane had come from. It was the safest place to hide. For ten years none of the other farmers – who surrounded me then, as they did in the war – would speak to me. They were all pilots and tank men from the war and hated all Germans, even us kids. All those years, I would cower on the floor beside the bed in Canada as the dark seethed at the window and the whole house was alive. And love. It came to me. Love. Standing at the window as the elms outside tore and thrashed at the moon. The shadows whipped over the house and over my face, and my language was nothing. It was lost to me. I was no one I knew. I was the silence.

I fingered the paint on the edge of the door, as Maryushka sang softly in the kitchen a Russian song. You did not need words – it was just a love song – a love that had to go away.

15. Two Christmases

@ The Christmas Drink

When I was a boy I woke suddenly and stumbled downstairs. All the lights were on. The family was singing around the tree, wearing old tattered clothes, their cheeks brightly scrubbed, with a few stubs of candle in the silver candle-clips, and nothing under the tree, not even for the littlest children. A man walked in with a grey Riesling bottle full of beechnut oil. He trembled slightly when he saw me, then poured each of the children a glass of oil, waited for them to drink it, then poured a full glass for Mama. She tossed it back in one gulp, shaking. The man came over to me and lowered his voice:

'When the dam was blown up by the dive-bombers on the Murg, the Murg came down in a wave forty feet high. On top was a barn, with a stupid pig staring out of it. All around the barn the water was straw and pieces of houses, and dead cows, or cows just swimming, their eyes big and white, and in the middle of it that stupid pig, staring out, wondering what was wrong. You heard it first as a big roar. It just kept coming, and growing louder and louder.'

That man was me. I wipe my eyes of sleep and step through the door into the kitchen. It is Christmas. Everyone has gone to church through the snow. I walk through the ghosts of the room.

Only Dorothy, my wife, and I are left. Shit, forgive my mind for wandering away. It scares me. It feels as if there has been no life between these years: fifty years ago I pushed open the door to the kitchen and now, fifty years later, I step into the room, and there is nothing, absolutely nothing, in between – all the people are gone, that boy is gone. Hansel. Maryushka is gone. Where to, I have no idea. Mama is gone, and I do not know them any more; all those years are gone. Now it is only scraps before me, and no world holding it together – the same room, only the people are gone. I feel drunk, but I have had nothing to drink. I do not know those people any more. They seem small and tired. It is cold in this big old house. Before, it was never so cold, this big, cold old house. The wind scares me, and time, that has torn us all to shreds: Mama is dead now; my language, and this town, this *house* are old and strange to me and I can hardly speak them. The snow is deep outside. The stars are crisp and cold, so clear and hard. There are a few sparks running up over the houses by the church. The whole world is made of ice. Stripped itself down. Frozen.

Tonight I do not know why I ever left, why I went to Canada, to farm. Those wide open spaces, why did I go there? Farming, so there was food, and you did not need the government? Back then, after that useless war, that war of stupidity and hate. But leave it, that is enough. You can speak too much about war.

∞∞∞

◈ A Walk in the Snow

I hear Dorothy's steps behind me, and turn. The fear is in me. I clench and unclench my fists in my pockets, trying to drive the tears from my eyes. She does not see it, or she sees it maybe but does not say so, thanks for that. She has always been full of mercy as I stood shaking and sweating in the dark with the wind over the house in that windy, dry valley of brush and gravel in Canada with the two children in their beds crying out in their sleep, poisoned by my dreams – the wind roaring over the roof like over the fuselage of a plane and the house shaking all around me. She always had her small mercies. That is my shame.

She has her coat on now and passes me my scarf and that big, clumsy toque she knitted. How can I tell her it embarrasses me to wear it here – everyone looking at me? She laughs, silly, like a bird – like a little girl.

'Stand still!' She helps me with it, as if I were a child, and I stand there; I stand there perfectly still. 'Shit,' I say. 'Let's get going. Come on, woman!' She winces at that, turns suddenly cold. I snatch the scarf from her and finish it roughly by myself and step out the back door. She comes right after me and together we step into the courtyard, with the night blowing in over us.

This is hard for her, too. I do not remember it being so cold since the war. The pear tree against the shed looks brittle and sharp. It is completely overgrown. Slowly, we crunch through snow that has melted and refrozen many times, with a hard glaze of ice. Dorothy is like a small sparrow under my arm. 'Cheer up, woman,' I say, pressing her close to me, and feel all her bones shift and grind under my arm. 'Are you OK?' 'I'm cold,' she says. Her voice seems small and distant – as if it is coming from far away. The stars shine in a frozen, black sky; there is no wind, only a great puffing cold searing through our coats from the end of the earth: never any sun any more, just the cold, and the snow queen there with the ice-flakes swirling over her face, so cold and blue that when I was a lit-tle boy I could not sleep, because she was there when I closed my eyes. There is no more world. The wind tears right through us, and stings our faces. But, God, it is beautiful here in the middle of the night, with the dark shoulders of the houses and above them the old stars and our frozen breath. We travel through all places and they change, and there is nothing that ties them together except us. It is not that it is all one place and things change – every moment in life is a different place and we stumble through them, trying to remember something, anything, of where we are or have been. But it is dark and beautiful in the night. There is nothing else but this, I think, looking up. 'It is beautiful,' I say to her. She shakes and rus-tles inside her coat. 'It's cold,' she answers.

The snow crunches. I look for storks, but there are none: of course, they have all flown south. But I remember them: white, like the stars, storks flapping and sailing like young girls overhead, all that strength in their wings, the whole wind moving with them. That is what used to get the year moving – a tough job. Ja, this is all there is, and the smell of stone in the streets.

<hr>

@ Pure Earth

When we get to the main street, where the army trucks used to drive, there is still no wind, but there are the scraps and rags of one, and coarse, gritty drifts, half sand, half snow. It is Christmas Eve, and no traffic has passed. The snow is shovelled out in front of the two inns, scraped down to the bricks of the sidewalks and thrown out in rough piles. Every window is a black, empty frame filled only with one white candle. As we move up the street, the flames look like people. Our shadows flare briefly against the snow, large and twisted, quickly sweeping out from us. When I look up a side alley into Old Town, it is not there! There are only a few old houses, Franzel's, sure, and Rudi's, but not the old, twisted cobbled streets. With the wind freezing my ears, I stand there and put my arms around my shoulders and hug myself, and shiver. My face is stiff with ice.

'What's wrong?' she asks. 'We're going to be late.'

'It does not matter,' I say. 'It does not make any difference if we are late. I have not been to church since I was a boy and then it meant little. It was just something I did.'

Life had order to it. I could recognize order. Now it just seems wild and strange.

∞∞∞

A Sooty Crow

When we reach the square in front of the church we are so cold that Dorothy is white as starlight seen through a glass of sour wine. There are some boys there, dressed in clothes like the ones we wore fifty years ago, doing something in the shadows. As we walk closer, we see a big flare of light, and I know what they have done. Dorothy tenses, startled: it is a tree, a *Tanne* from the forest; at the top the boys have tied a wooden crow, and they have hung stars of straw and cornsilks from the branches: it is all on fire – bright, crackling. All of a sudden the door of the church bursts open and the father steps out in his black robe, with the light flowing over him into the night from the warmth.

'Come into the church!' he calls.

At his voice, the boys scatter. Suddenly I realize, with Dorothy shivering at my side, I am one of those boys! It is impossible, yet I cannot shake the idea from my head! But I do not remember the tree.

The tree burns quickly. Soon there are only a few thin threads of smoke leaking from the tip of each twig. Black as a shadow, the charred crow falls. I bend down and grab it in my rough, farmer's hand. It is warm, and I clench it in my pocket. The father is still standing in the door. His shadow leaps forward from him, and over the walls of the houses across the street, and up into the stars, catching a few flakes of snow beginning to form out of the air. With the light shining on him from behind, the father's face is a shadow.

As we step into the yellow light, the warmth floods over us, wet with melted snow from people's boots. I quickly pull off the toque and stuff it into my pocket, then unwind the scarf from my neck. Candles have been set in fir boughs along the walls, and more wreaths on the ends of each of the dark, polished pews. The building is still harsh and stark, though – everything sharp and stark and crisp, filled with a cruel, stern light, without dimension. You cannot breathe.

As we stand there, puffing, the father closes the huge oak doors behind us with a bang, and as the sound echoes loudly through the whole church, every face in the church turns back to look at us – white faces with cheeks red from beer and cold.

My legs are weak, and Dorothy is beside me, as I start walking to the front – to the family pew. Damn. They are all there. All my brothers are there, and my sisters; they have all come to welcome me home. It does not feel like home. Dorothy whispers 'Gute Nacht' to everyone we pass. I nod stiffly and bunch up my scarf in my hand. The father's footsteps follow me. Suddenly, I see my father! He steps in the door – back from the war; 1945; he sees a little baby, and my stepfather there. For three years we thought Papa was dead. Papa does not come in; he turns on his heel and puts on his hat, so carefully, and walks out the door.

My brothers, Volker and Michel and Eberle, dressed in black, with white shirts and thin black ties, all stand to shake my hand. They have grown older, too. We all look old and pale. I do not remember them like this. It is wrong. I pull my hand from my pocket. It is black with soot. I reach it out to my first brother, Michel, but when I see it there I pause, and put it out no farther: it is a rough, scarred hand, calloused and hard and black, like a claw. Michel sees it too, but he just laughs and grabs it and shakes it – limply. He has a limp handshake! Then my other brothers shake it in turn, their breath rich with chocolate and wine, laughing. Their handshakes are all soft, just a touch and a sliding away. I look over and Margot smiles at me with her thin, dark lips. My beautiful sister, you are growing old. Dammit, we are all growing old; what is to become of us! It is as if we are prisoners. I smile back. I hope she does not see that I am afraid. I hope nobody sees. I do not want anyone to see it.

oooooooooooooooooooooooooooooooooooooooooooooooooooooooooooooooooooooooooooooooooooooooooooooo

▨ The Sermon of the Stars

When the father walks up to the front, I stare up at him like a small boy, with my face shiny and my hair slicked back. He grasps the pulpit in his hands and begins to talk. We sit in neat rows before him, smelling like wet wool and wet leather, small in those big, hard pews.

'The stars you walked under tonight are the first stars. Above our houses is the first night of God.'

Shit, what does he know! He is so young – he did not go through that time. What does he know.

'We want to get back to the stars, to that cold, pure, and pitiless space without judgement. Jesus cast down the hypocrites, for he did not need hypocrites – he did not need ways of doing things that were created by men!'

The father looked up. All of us in the church were fidgeting in our seats.

'It seems at first that we have only this approach, only this movement towards God, but Heaven is a place, scattered all around us. All things are all around us, all in the same places, all at the same time. When we leave this church, when all of us have left, it is full of wind. It is not filled with silence. It is a roaring, surging wind. I cannot prove it – when I am here to see the wind, there is no wind – but still I know it is here. I know it is here, but it is vanity to live by talking about that breath and to live for our words. We are not God enough.'

All the time that he spoke people grew restless – but my eyes were riveted on him. Where had he been when I was a boy! Because when I was a boy all I saw was the silence. Except once. Once it was stripped away.

As I was coming up the street a voice filled the air and I saw a cloudy breath before me – I could not see anybody or anything, there was only the light before me. Then I heard inside the air.

There was the clatter of automatic rifle fire, and the sound of high, thin voices screaming. The breath grew hotter on my face, and the voice barked out, 'Archangel!' The one called Archangel answered, 'Yes, my Lord.' The one who was breathing on me threw me to the cobbles, and snapped, 'What is this?' The archangel kicked me with a hard boot and laughed, 'It is a boy!' 'Get him out of here.' Suddenly I was yanked up. His breath was right in my face, so I could feel it in my lungs when I breathed. It tasted like sweet flowers, like clover nectar. It was so choked with pollen that it made me cough. Then I saw his eyes, a deep brown goat's eyes. They were incredibly sad. He spoke again, except I could taste the words when they came out, but not hear them. 'You can only be hot.' Then he vanished. But the sound of the rifle fire did not go away.

I got up panting, with heavy soot all over me, my lips yellow from pollen and – of all things! – a book in my hand. I opened it. There were ashes in it, nothing more. The ashes sifted out. I threw the book away. I brushed the ashes off my hands and went up to Franzel's, trying to wipe my hands off on my pants as I walked. Franzel did not really want us boys there, but she did not chase us away either. I helped her make cheese, hanging the curds in the cheese cloth, and she did not ask. She did take a cloth out of her pocket and spit on it, and wiped the pollen off my swollen lips. It was as if she kissed me. She looked me straight in the face, and she said, 'I would be careful who I talked to.'

∞∞

⁀ A Drink of Beechnut Oil

I stumble down from the cold bed in the morning. Dorothy is still up there, curled into the eiderdown, breathing the frost, trying to drive out the cold by holding perfectly still. When I push open the door at the bottom of the stairs, my eyes are still cloudy and thick with the dead sludge of dreams. In a corner by the piano there is a Christmas tree, with a few stubs of candle, and with a tinsel angel – the tip of the tree tucked in under her skirts. There is a family there, gathered around the tree. It is my family – it is 1944! Mama too! All my brothers and sisters are dressed in grubby, worn-out clothes. I step suddenly back out of the way: there is a boy, twelve years old, coming from the kitchen. He steps around me into the front room, a glass in one hand, an old wine bottle full of beechnut oil in the other. I stand back in the shadows. My hair is thinning. I have farmer's hands and bloodshot cheeks. I do not belong here. I am a stranger. The boy comes into the room and pours each of my brothers and sisters a glass of oil as the snow spatters against the window. At the end the boy pours a glassful for Mama. She tosses it back in one gulp, sits down, and cries.

As I slouch back in the doorway, I hear Dorothy calling from upstairs. I turn for a moment to hear what she is saying, but I cannot catch it. When I turn back to the room everyone has gone. The room is bare, as if someone had come in with a putty knife and tried to scrape off all the light and had only bruised it and gouged it and marked it up. I go into the kitchen to wait for Dorothy. We will be late for church. The garden is tangled and overgrown. The snow is falling heavily out there in the dark, settling thickly against the sash. I cannot see much outside – the snow falling, in the shaft of light from the window, flake on flake on flake, little angels drifting on the wind. We try to find love and this is what we find: a world drowning.

16. Sabotage and Retreat

The Bridge

Rudi and I were crawling through the soggy fields, down through the fog to the river, and through black hedges like dark walls of water, the thick fog turning to drops in the air. We came to the slick, black shore and the gravel, then the river stretching out as if it had eaten its own shadow, river and shadow moving all at once, cold and smoky, tasting of oil and eels and gravel and mud. We crawled through the bunker under the huge crow-shadows of the bridge. There was nothing else, just that taste.

The soldiers had wired the bridge – there were no more bullets; nothing to stop the French except to blow up the bridge. Rudi and I thought it was crazy, absolutely crazy.

'Come on,' I said to him. 'Let's cut the wires.'

We crawled along through the bushes and broken bits of concrete. The bridge was above us, cutting out the sky. We could hear the clatter of soldiers loading their trucks. When a truck drove off the bridge above us the whole bridge was a loud roar, as if it was the truck. I told Rudi to wait, and climbed up the iron rungs on the pillar, out of the flood-broken scrub. If they had seen me there, or heard the clang of my feet on the rungs – if they had shut off their trucks, and stopped sliding their stuff in, they would have heard me, but I hugged close to the concrete, as the wind began to tug at me, testing me, and they did not see.

High in the air, I hung off the side of the bridge and cut through the detonation wire, even while the trucks were pulling away, their headlights hooded. When I had finished, I climbed slowly back down the rungs. When the wind tugged at me I was almost weightless. I got down to Rudi, and we got out of there quickly through the scrub.

Trigonometry

It was foggy all the way back to town. When Rudi and I came across the bomb craters and blasted sand and twisted concrete and metal, even whole trucks lying burnt up and twisted in the sand and fog, I told Rudi how we had come from the camp up in the forest. The soldiers had given us some of their *Eintopf*. You just have one pot. If you have anything, everything you have you just throw in there. You all ate out of there, with hard black bread. We thought it was the best stuff in the world.

We had to know trigonometry up in the forest. I had to quit going to music! I used to go down to Schreiber's basement in Rastatt. He had a piano – out of tune, with three keys that did not play anything at all, and if you played on any of the keys the dust came puffing up! It was blistered by the rain, had fallen right through the floors when the bombs fell – some old lady's thing! Ja, Schreiber laughed. He found a china dog of hers, too – a little white poodle! And a strange old thing – 'That is a corset,' he laughed. A whalebone corset. He drank some more beer, really quickly, and set those old things up on the piano. They were there whenever he played. They shook a little. A poodle and a whalebone corset.

He played music for us in his small, dark, dusty basement, with the tiles blown off the roof by bombs, the rooms upstairs empty and busted up. He played the Emperor Concerto. He liked to show us how fast he could play through it – over and over and over, faster and faster. Flying! Ja, Schreiber. I guess he was not that old, really. He had been up in Moscow, and had shoes made of rope, I do not know, but he played music for us. He was drunk mostly.

I had to go to trigonometry class instead. For a whole month I did nothing but trigonometry – I learned to hate it, but it got me into camp. It was not a Hitler Youth Camp but a training camp for the younger boys, ten years old. We lived in tents, on hard bunks. We slept with nothing on, with no sheet, under one thin wool blanket. It was cold. Of course we did not sleep much. They sent us shooting – into the trees! We had classes in just about everything, hammering with the left hand, working with the left hand, you know, in case we got busted up in the war. We learned all the kinds of aircraft, everything about guns, how to sight the big guns, how to take a rifle apart and grease it, how to put it back together. We studied German too, and Hebrew, ha, everything you could think of, Hebrew – ja, can you imagine that! – up there in the Black Forest. All we had to eat was *Eintopf*. We just had a big black pot and we threw everything into it. We scraped it off our plates with a dry heel of bread. Maybe we threw in a cow's head, and there would be ugly, yellow grease floating on top. We ate that, with hair in it too. We soaked it up into that bread. It was cold. We sat around shivering.

My Career as a Pilot

Every morning at camp we had to run naked two miles down to a creek and wash in icy mountain water, without soap, then run back, when the shadows were still thick and cold on the ground. That is where we made the trips from, to the bunkers, to see how the war was fought, how you did it! We came in the back of trucks, sitting on top of loads of lumber. They had Poles logging in the forest, and gypsies at gunpoint. They taught us to fly gliders. That was a mess. I crashed the damn thing – into a field, with a couple of stupid, sick-looking cows. They looked at me strangely, too! I still have the scar. It was just soaring, with the wind tugging at the glider, only the wind. Shit, I felt really free up there, then I crashed the bastard.

How I Left the Camp

When I left the camp I was on an orienteering exercise, alone in the forest with a compass and a knife. I had to walk across several valleys. I did not know where I was in the thick bush, but I had to come back, without getting lost. They did not give me anything to eat. That was my problem.

On my second day, I saw planes through the branches of the trees, the firs and beeches and pines that bent up in the wind, the hazels and the scrub bushes, swimming and dark and dizzy. The shocks rolled through the ground when the bombs hit, then the rumble of the explosions poured through the trees. The birds burst out of the branches around me, as if God was beating his rugs with a stick.

When I got to camp, with big welts on my bare legs and face, and my eyes burning because I had walked into small dead twigs on the hazel bushes, the smoke had already blown away. There was nothing left. The tents were blown up. There were bodies everywhere. Flies sat on my friends' eyes. Everyone was dead. I could not tell who they were, just that they had been my friends and then they were dead. That is where I learned that in this war everyone dies. You die one way or another way. We were all stupid dead people.

It was a hundred kilometres, but I walked home through the forest, and then through the fields. I got there on all the back mountain roads. Nobody stopped me. I just had a few butternuts to eat, and a few wormy apples from the ditches. There were no berries. I could spend the night in a barn and steal some milk. Mama was surprised to see me. All my other brothers and sisters were up at Pforzheim for safety. Michel had a flak gun by this time, on the Rhine, so I was the only one home, and that was alright by Mama.

17. Defeat

The Retreat

The French were just over the river. The fields were empty. There were no more army trucks on the road, only soldiers staggering north. The women spat at them from their windows, right through the geraniums, as they plodded beneath them with the odd horse, and maybe a horse pulling a truck. The men were dirty and their uniforms were faded and worn out. Maryushka turned away when she saw them, in their worn boots tied together with string, half asleep, tall guys slumped over, their guns hanging off them and banging as they marched. Some of them had boots so worn that the soles were flapping against their feet. There were men with bloody, greasy bandages around their heads, marching, men with only one eye or their face twisted and burnt, their fingers melted together, staggering, with soot on their cheeks – as if they had come out of a hole in the ground and were walking across town, and were going into another hole, and no one would ever see them again; as if they were already dead. Sometimes some things are too real.

The Firebombing of the Rose Garden

Mama and Blaumann got married in the town hall, with a white wreath of flowers for Mama and a red armband for Blaumann. The next week, the French started shelling us with little firebombs. The bombs had a fuse in them, so they would sit for a half minute before they exploded. They were made of phosphorus, so you could not put them out. We saw them coming across the field, small bursts of fire that burned even in that wet grass. We dragged ourselves out of bed to watch. The shells quickly came closer, and Blaumann grabbed me and took me upstairs. 'Follow me!' he yelled.

We went into the attic. The shells smashed through the roof tiles with a crack. One by one we picked them up and threw them out the attic window into the rose garden. Not one of them went off in the house! The shelling went on for three hours and not one of them went off in the attic! We saved the house. Other houses all over town were burning, and our garden was on fire, but we let it

burn out. Where all those bombs landed it was years before anything would grow. Not even the weeds would grow there. The fire
crackled like poison, burning on itself, boiling.

We saved our house, but the tiles were smashed off the roof.
Anyone could look at Papa's bird-hunting rifles, which he had hidden there before the war. He had us children crawl in those small
spaces in the dark. It was against the law to have guns of any kind,
but Papa kept them – shotguns and old blunderbusses with big
wide barrels, for ducks, his boar rifles too – for the times we
thrashed through the bush and chased the boars into a clearing and
he shot them. We took the guns quickly back into the basement.
The tiles were all broken to bits and it was a long time before we
got more tiles to put in their place.

<hr>

⊛ The Smell of the Church

I was at church when the French came. Some of the police went
into the church that day, smelling of Cologne water, beef fat, and
dog-shit from their boots. Tante Anna came too, with bundles of
dried alder cones from the scrub in the forest. The alder cones
smelled like rain and moss. Her skin smelled like the dry paper of a
hornet's nest. Her hair smelled of musty straw.

Bernd came in, smelling of lard. He had found a supply of lard at
last! It was terrible grey stuff, already half soap, cakes wrapped in
paper that said Soap. It was sent to the police in town, but they
would not use it – when they lathered it onto their skin it smelled
burnt. It was greasy and thick – moved the dirt around on their skin,
but did not strip it off! Once a week a motorcycle courier made a spe-
cial trip to bring them more. When Bernd came to their barracks, the
police gave it to *him!* They were laughing as they dumped it into his
two tin lard buckets. He was about to leave when the door blew
open after him and the police threw a whole box of it into the street.
The hard cakes scattered over the cobbles – like bricks of margarine.
Bernd bundled it all back together and slowly limped home. Maybe
he had only a little lye left, but he had a supply of soap now! There in
his kitchen, stuffing wood into his old green-tiled stove where he

used to sit warming his feet, he cooked up the soap. He tried to render it back to lard, but it would not melt. He did manage to cook out the smell of burnt hair – one day the smell flooded down through the streets of Old Town, heavier than air, lying close to the ground. The closer it came to us in New Town, the less of a smell it became and the more the sound of people calling out, afraid, until it ran out into the field, swept away by the wind, and lifted up. A gritty rain spattered over us, throwing sand against the windows, grinding at the paint and stucco. Suddenly all our houses looked old. At the same time, the black imprint of a cross appeared on the door of the church. The next day it had spread and covered the entire door: the Black Door. It frightened us children. The Black Door was intensely cold when you pushed against it, so black it was darkness itself. When you get really afraid, things are exactly themselves.

With his pot of pure clean soap that smelled of chamomile and rosewater Bernd came into the church. He set the pot of soap down before the altar. It smelled of women stepping out of a bath, rubbing oil over their skin. Bernd smelled of ashes and fire. His face was grey – as if his heart had stopped.

Franzel came in that day too. Everyone turned to look at her when they heard her footsteps: a sea of white faces, twisted, grim and dirty. She came into the church smelling of hay in a field under the sun. She had flecks of straw in her greasy, uncombed hair. She came in with her little boy, Daniel. He was crying. He smelled of salt.

'The French are coming,' Franzel said at last, standing there. 'No one is shelling them. The army has just left.'

We should have asked why. We thought we knew. We thought it was the French. It was not. It was worse. It was the darkness inside ourselves, that part of our selves that we cannot answer.

Father Thomas smelled of sour wine, a shrill high note, a piercing woodwind of a smell above the orchestra of smells in that old church. I stank of onions. It filled the whole church – like a violin shriek.

We were all a song.

☙ The Choir of the Dead

The police tore off their jackets and kicked off their boots, but it was no use: the war was coming on us too quickly. Tante Anna looked at them like a rock. The light at the window was flat light that the windows had made of the sun – light that had skipped the world and had come straight from God! It grew very bright and sharp – and there in the stew of smells were the dead, some snarling and crawling over the floor, some as dull, grey shapes in the pews around us, filling the church. It was so crowded they had to stand in the back, their faces grim and expressionless, revealing nothing. Sitting on the windowsill above us were two of God's angels the colour of sulphur – bright like scraps of fire that had condensed inside the dimensionless light. They wavered and burnt like candle flames. They were like ideas, but in that flattened light you could see them: thick ideas. Everything else in the whole room was flat – so that is how you could see them. Because the light stuck to them and they kept growing thicker and brighter, they sat up there, looking down at us. Under their stares, the police forgot what they were doing. It was completely washed from their heads! They forgot who they were and stumbled out the door, shaking their heads a little, laughing. We never saw them again. They were washed clean. We were being washed away into the silence. Everything was going so quickly.

☙ The Drowning of the Angels

The soap grew heavy with light, too, and when the light in the church grew thick enough, the soap became a young woman and a baby. The woman had no clothes on at all. She was glowing. The light beaded on her like cold water. With shaking hands, Father Thomas laid his old wool sweater with big knotted leather buttons over her shoulders. The woman walked to the back of the church. When she stepped through the open doors, the whole choir of smells poured out of the door after her; all the grey dead ghosts stepped out scared, carefully, slowly, with her at their head. The light hurt their eyes – they squinted and turned their eyes away for a second, frightened like little children, before stepping out towards the edge of the square. The farther they went the thinner they grew in front of us, until they passed out of our lives forever. It was days before the police were found again, hiding in Franzel's barn!

With the doors open, a sparrow flew into that swirling light that was half the flattened-out light of God, as if you had pounded it with a hammer, and half the sunlight pouring in with the fresh air through the door. With the police gone we felt lighter. The church was half empty. It smelled of wood and varnish and sweat.

The sparrow flew up high from one end of the church to the other, looking for a way out. The angels called to it. One of them leaped off the stone casement to catch it and to soothe it, and was tossed around on the boiling light like a swimmer caught in white river rapids. The other angel jumped out to save the first one, but it was useless. Suddenly the church was empty, the light was dull and old, the pews were old and chipped, with dark shadows under them. Our world was gone. In the dead quiet a bird was smashing itself against the window, again and again, where the light poured in weakly, broken up by the glass. The wings of the bird threw large, dull shadows over us.

That is how Father Thomas got angels in his church. When he found the soap again and slipped it into his pocket it was hot. In the months and years after that if anybody hurt or crying came into the church, Father Thomas would put out a bowl of water and a bar of soap, and say, 'Wash it away.' After they had washed, people would step out of the church again, and see the light as light and wood as wood. They would be clean at last.

Even so, something went out of our lives when that young woman led all the dead out of town towards the French army. Everything became flat and empty. Sure, a lot of people went looking for the dead, all over, in the woods outside of town, in the bushes and ditches and on the roads, but they were never found. They had simply disappeared. We could tell, even then, as the light cooled all around us: some strength had gone out of our lives. Everything was real at last, but it was only one thing and you could not move between things any more. And there was no more silence.

Then there was the sound of trucks, a shaking of diesel engines rumbling up through the floor. We all knew: the French were here. The light had vanished from the room. We got up. We did not know what we had come to church to find. We ran out into the street, like drops of water scurrying away from a dropped stone, into a puddle full of sky.

18. Protection and Imprisonment

ⓖ Daniel

When the war lashed its tail and struck, I was hurrying home down my long, empty street. I heard a scream, and whirled around – I saw the terrible thing that ruined Franzel: a hundred feet away the first French truck rolled into town; the driver swerved, the white teeth burning in his black face – a Moroccan! They had sent the bloody Moroccans against us! Those black bastards! He ran right over Franzel's boy. The truck lurched as it went over him, the driver laughed, Daniel lay there in the street, his chest crushed, blood spilled out of his mouth, and Franzel screamed. Ja, we do not have grief in this world any more. This is a world washed clean, without grief, or love, or any goddamn thing, but we still had echoes of it then. That is the way words die. They wither away. Like people do. We still had a little grief left, then. The wind stuck right to you. You could not feel it as wind. It made you irritable; carrying it around, you wanted to throw it off, but you did not know what you wanted to throw off! Ja. Shit. Franzel did not know what she was doing. She ran out into the street and grabbed the boy, and almost got rammed by the next truck.

Franzel slumped down in the shadows of Meyer's doorway. Across the street, Frau Schmidt came out, wiping her hands on her apron, and Meyer came out. He looked at the French trucks, then turned back inside. I ran away, with a silent place in my chest, my blood pooling in something empty where my heart used to be. When I got home I jumped up the steps. The sound of the door opening was like a rifle shot. I slammed it shut behind me.

'Hansel, is that you?'

'Mama!' I called back.

I came in to her, pale and out of breath. I told her. The French had come. They had run over Daniel. She was sitting there in the dark. In that grey light, she said, 'Hansel, now you have to be brave. There will be nothing now. But do not hate them. Hate is a poison. Do not take the hate into yourself. We either live or hate. Do you understand that?'

Not at all. Not in my sleep or at any time.

She was right. Except for those goddamn Moroccans. Shit, I hated them. Mama was always down at the hospital. She never saw our life up here in the town, just the empty roads she walked every day to the hospital in her white coat, hunched over against the rain and the wind; the empty streets with the echoes of her footsteps blowing around her, the dead people lying in the doorways – coughing, or moaning in pain – where they slept wrapped in a bunch of old rags; her footsteps echoing right around her. Sometimes one of her footsteps blew in front of her face. So she did not know.

I hated those black bastards. They sprouted up out of the dirt. You saw them in the magazines, all dirty and smoking cigarettes, just trash sitting around in an old field, just the garbage they sent against us. Every bit of me was a bit more hate for them – even my elbow or my cheekbone. Ja! But Mama was right – it made me weak. I was scared and helpless. So I walked around like a nightmare, not somebody who was alive.

We read those magazines because there was nothing else – that is what the government gave us – hate. You could not look to the country for anything. If you wanted anything you had to look within yourself to find it, but you did not know what to find, because all that was there was this hate they taught you, and then those bastards from Morocco did what they did and it seemed true after all, really true, just as we lost the war and I hated them and I hated myself for being a man, because there was nothing I could do – I was powerless. That is the worst. To us, being a man meant you had power, because that is what we grew up in, but we had nothing.

∞∞

◈ Waiting for Our Lives to Begin

We had never had lives – our fathers were at war, or they were dead, so what you learn from your fathers is dead stuff; you do not get a few bucks and the farm, or a cat wearing tall leather boots, who cracks jokes – only death. In all those long awful nights when Mama and I were alone in that big house we would sit together on the edge of my bed, watching the snow sift through the cracks around the window. You could only feel the emptiness out there, with the weight of the stars heavy on you. The whole world was empty. There was not a thing left in it: it was all gone.

oooooooooooooooooooooooooooooooooooooooooooooooooooooooooooooooooooooooooooooooooo

@ Visitors

There was the sound of trucks in the street, and banging and shouting. 'You stay here,' Mama said. Her eyes had gone clear and blue,
as if they were two tears in her head. She rose quickly from her seat
and ran to the door. There were two French soldiers there, but
before they could smash their way in with the butts of their rifles,
Mama opened the door and said very politely, 'Bonjour, Messieurs.
Soyez les bienvenus à ma maison. Comment ça va?' They just
stared at her. All up and down the street soldiers were kicking in
the doors, and there was shouting and screaming, but these two
just stood there and very quickly said, so politely, 'Bonjour,
Madame, excusez-nous.' And they left! In a few minutes the whole
street was full of smashed glass. The sound of trucks came down
from Friedrichstraße, but not like it used to, flowing out of the old
part of town like mountain water. This sound came down empty
and thin. It was just simply there. You could tell the distance in it.
You could never do that with the sound before. Now you could.
Mama closed the door, and sat down on the hall bench. She kicked
off her shoes. Then she looked up. She saw the painting of our
Leader in the hall – we had grown so used to seeing it there we had
forgotten to hide it or bury it in the garden.

'Hansel, you have forgotten the picture!'

I looked up. Our Leader was staring straight at me. It must have
been the last painting like that in all of Germany! He was black
and white and huge. What were we going to do about him then!

We did not have time to decide. I had buried everything in our
old tunnel in the rose garden. But this I had forgotten.

When the door knocked again, I felt it knocking right inside of
me.

Mama glanced up at me. She hurried out to answer the door. We
did not know who it could be, who we had finally magicked up to
settle with us! She opened the door, her face pale and white from
working too much at the hospital, with the fighting. 'Bonjour,

Madame,' said the officer there.

The war was here.

<hr/>

☺ The Gift of Resistance

The French had looked all over town for us. Before he died, Pierre had contacted the Resistance, so the French army had come to protect Mama. They took over our house for their headquarters and locked us in the basement. They singled us out for this shame – to protect us! We did not tell the French soldiers what we knew – the world had changed into a different world. That is what the war had done. That is what the police wanted. All along we should have known that. That was the war. But we could not find the words.

Everything was smashed up. You walked around a corner and there was your great-great-grandmother killing chickens, crying as she did it. Everything was shrinking into itself. That is not strength. We were dribbling away, as if the change had been made, but out of nothing and on nothing, with nothing to sustain it, and we had missed the point where it had all happened because it had happened a little piece at a time – that part of ourselves was not there. There were pools of God all around, puddles on the cobbles, or something you would walk into – the air would smell of clouds and be intensely cold. The old gods had returned, but no one knew their names any more. The world was in pieces and scraps, like when you thresh grain in the wind and the wind lifts off the chaff. We did not tell the French that, though. We were too hungry to tell them anything, and not hungry enough yet to swallow our hunger because it was the only kind of food we were going to get.

<hr/>

☺ Shouting on the Moon

Right away, the French saw the picture of our Leader. The picture started to talk! It said, very loudly, that we were no good, we were weak, we should die. The lips grew redder and redder as it talked.

The French pulled it down and started searching the whole house for more stuff like it. They found Maryushka, and took her away, to send her back to Russia. The last I saw of her was her white hands, untying her apron. Then the French turned to us.

'You will have to go to jail,' said the soldiers. 'When we show this to the general, he will burn down your house!'

They left the picture leaning in the hallway while they searched the house.

'Hansel, do something!'

Our Leader was shouting loudly that we had been betrayed, that we were worth nothing, we were no better than dogs.

If an adult stole the picture, that would be serious, so I grabbed the picture and slipped outside – but there was a sentry! He found me as soon as I came around the back of the garage by the peach tree. He started to chase me. I was holding that big, stupid picture, and he was shouting after me, 'Arrête! Arrête-toi!' I threw the picture in the canal and ran into the neighbours' yard. The picture sank into the lead mud.

I snuck back at night through the window of the laundry room, a little window in the metre-thick sandstone. It was a good thing I had not eaten much, or I would never have squeezed through. From then on our house was a French house. The French never mentioned the painting again.

That night I dreamed of our Leader lying on the bottom of the canal as the red-headed canal fish swam over his face and little bubbles rose from his mouth. He was shouting that he had been betrayed, that we were worth nothing, we were no better than dogs, but it is like dropping a rock on the moon: if there is no air, and no one there to hear it, there is no sound. I dreamt it all night, and when I woke up the sky was blue.

19. The Starvation

⊚ Orange Peels

The officers cooked in our kitchen. They had meat, and fresh veg-
etables, and cheese, and oranges. Ja, oranges! They trucked them
all the way north to our town. One day a whole truckload of
oranges came in. The French gave them out on the street! For days
the streets had orange peels all over them! The smart people gathered up the peels. When they were dry they chewed them like
leather. One day a whole truckload of wine arrived from France.
That day the officers invited Mama up for a drink. She stayed there
with them for a long time, while we sat in the basement and
chewed on our orange peels: an orange sun.

∞∞

⊚ Eating Iron

We were starving. I stole food whenever I could. I would steal it
again. You cannot keep food from people. That is just too terrible.

One of the guards said, 'There is a truck on the road with
Wehrmacht iron rations. They taste awful. They must have
scraped them out of the bottom of a chicken pen!' I stood there in
my tire shoes and listened. I got the hint.

It took me four hours crawling to get to the truck and back.
There were guards around the house, guards around the truck, and
traffic always coming and going from our house, with lights beam-
ing into the yard, the slam of car doors, and sentries everywhere. I
got there through the hedge, centimetre by centimetre so I would
not make a noise in the dried leaves. It was a heavy box too – it
took all I had to drag it. A hundred metres!

I tapped on the coal window for Mama to open it. The house sentry found me. He was a tall man with a bald head. He grabbed the big
heavy box under one arm, took me by the wrist, and dragged me into
the dining room. I thought I was dead. My heart was beating hard,
and every time it beat the world went more slowly. The general was
smoking a cigar. His men looked up at me, sideways, from the table,
with all their papers and maps as I passed by. The general looked up,
too, bloodshot. The sentry told him. He stared at me for a long time,

with a cigar burning between his fingers, then he called up his aide and told him to make up a big plate of food for us, with pears and cheese and bread and meat. He gave it to me and gave me a bottle of wine, and said, 'If you get caught stealing food again, you will be shot.' Then he turned away, back to his papers!

The General's Wine

In the days after that, I would see Papa in the corner, in the shadows, unwinding bandages from his head. He would say those Russians come against you with a turnip in their pocket and a couple of bullets; that is all they needed – they could fight with that. Everything would be in black and white. I would bury my head in my pillow and cry, and bite the pillow, hard. We had heard that he was dead in Russia. The world felt like something you rip out of a newspaper.

I was spending most of my time in bed then, we all were, to keep our strength. In that basement there was nothing else to do. We could not go out and we could not go upstairs. The only time we were not bored was when one of the French soldiers came down with a plate of food. We were hungry, but it made us feel so helpless. I was away from Old Town, and I did not see much in my dreams any more. I did not need to. I did not realize they had escaped from me. Now they were real. I was nothing. I was not there. That is what I did not realize about that time. I thought it was the world that was disappearing. I was wrong. It was me. We were all being changed into something new.

The French soldier brought meat and bread and a bottle of wine, and left it with us. Every time he would say, 'Madame, the general has sent you a bottle of wine.'

Every time – every single time. He did that.

Once he even left us with that box of German rations, but we did not touch them – we were saving them for when the French left and we would get really hungry.

⑥ Mercy

When they came for Mama they would come down quickly, their boots tromping on the steps. They would take her into town to doctor someone who was sick. As I was the man of the house, I would go along. The town was completely changed. I saw no one I knew. Those people I saw were hurrying quickly from one house to another. Everywhere there were French soldiers, like tourists with guns. It was strange to have all those black men there, in our town. They were like devils, just as they used to teach us in magazines – that they were not people. Now we were not people.

It was just a town of children and women and old men. There was nothing else – the Allies had not started sending back the German prisoners yet; Uncle Hans had not come back yet with TB; Grandma had not come home – they all had not come back to die in our house. That is all our house was then – it was alive once but it had become the end: a coffin. Michel had not come back from the POW camp. Whenever we saw Father Thomas he looked paler and weaker than the time before. Everything was just dwindling away. The strength was going out of everything.

The war threw us out of our selves into the world. Now it was throwing us out of the world. How could you stop it? Nothing was real as we say things are real now, in Canada.

∞∞∞

⑥ The Death of the Old Ones

When Tante Anna died, the cows stood still and silent in their stalls and gave no milk for a week. Mama and I went up then, and again when Bernd died and suddenly the rats had come creeping out of the houses and the blown-up bricks of the trainyard and rushed into the square, hundreds of them! Many of them drowned in the fountain. Sometimes there would be a new baby. I would have to help Mama with that, too, and had to wash it off for her. Getting out and going into town never lasted long, though – I got out, my eyes adjusted to the light, I could see it clearly, then I was in the basement again, in the choking dark, going blind. The light hurt. It burned right into my brain without being changed into an image of what I was looking at. It was just the pure, harsh, burning, acid light of God, and only slowly could I see it. I had to learn to see the world. It was too bright.

<hr />

◉ Amnesia

Papa found me even in my dreams. He had not yet awoken in a French army hospital to suddenly remember who he was, and had not yet come home to find Blaumann and a new baby in his house. I did not know what he was trying to say. He was trying to give me some sort of message, but I could not understand. The dead talk to you. They have so much they would like to talk to you about, but they say it through being dead and not through living things. When they are really doing well, then it is through living things, but as they remember it. They do not remember it very well! Every time Papa came he was more and more upset. After a while he did not look like he knew who I was at all any more. Then he seemed to forget who he was too. At first he lost his colour. Then he grew thinner and thinner. Then he did not come any more at all.

20. Hell

@ The Rape

The officer stood there with the grey light of the basement flickering around him, licking at his clothes and settling down on us like dust.

'It is the Maria next door. My men will be punished. Right now would the Madame Doctor just come, would she just put the girl back together again, merde.' His face was drawn and tired. 'You had to understand. An army needs punishment. It was not our job to hurt you. The men will be punished, but right now, first, I had to ask you to come to the girl. She has lost a lot of blood. It is very ugly.'

My mother looked at him there with the grey light sinking into the pores of his face. She nodded, and placed her hand around my shoulder. 'Come, Hansel. I need you there.'

We made our way under the stars. They were leaves fluttering on the surface of a stream above us as our whole lives flowed away over us, the stars rocking and tossing in the current. We were fish on the bottom of a river. For the first time I felt it was all flowing away. God had his eye on this world. He was stripping the whole world off, and all of time, to get to us, to see us, and he was very close. Then I knew if God does not want to be seen, he will not. He will be the dark, and you will see stars through it. But if he really saw us, down somewhere where we do not have our bodies but are only coals dying from a fire, there would be no stars. We would be walking alone, and everything, everything around us, would be empty, and that was the face of God.

The wind and the dark of the night blew over us, down the streets of the town, and our clothes fluttered and snapped at us, and our bodies flickered and almost went out.

The barracks was a barn up in the old part of town. As we stepped into it a few slates were torn off the roof by the wind and smashed down at our feet. For a moment we could see nothing; it was dark in there, and there was no sound.

'Turn on a light,' Mama said. 'I cannot work in the dark.'

The officer said some French. A man stepped out of the shadows and gave us a flashlight. That is how we found Maria. She was in the straw at the back. The thin beam of the flashlight cut thinly through the dark, as if we were miles underwater: a crazy, wobbling flash of light, splashing around in front of us, mimicking our footsteps, spraying all over the walls in the scent of mildew and stale old air and piss – air that has been there for centuries! Centuries of cows and shit. Then another smell – the smell of hot dust and semen: Africa! Then Maria, lying in the straw, with a blanket thrown over her – an old horse blanket, from the French army. The smell of blood.

'Hold the flashlight,' Mama said. 'Hold it as steady as you can where I am working. You have to be a man for me here.'

Maria had no clothes. She was bruised and weak and bleeding, and her cunt was raw meat, and I held my light on it. Mama clenched her teeth together and scrunched up her shoulders. The officers turned away, swearing, stood by the door, smoking thin cigarettes, and stared out into the paler dark beyond the doorway. With a sound like a thousand horses passing through the street at full gallop the tiles were ripping off the roof and smashing on the cobbles like water thrown into water, going back to themselves, rock going to rock. I held the light so still. Maria's cheeks were blue and puffy, her breath was very thin. Her neat blond hair that always had those ribbons in it was tangled up and ground into the greasy wool blanket. That is what men could do. I saw that right there, damn it. I held the light on it, even though I was shaking, as Mama tried to keep the life from leaking out of Maria, and the whole building was shredding around us, smashing up.

As I held that thin yellow beam of light on Maria, her breathing slowed and grew more and more shallow. A thin light came into her face, as if her breathing could not keep up, as if something inside her was walking away. Her breaths struggled after it, but could not keep pace, and Mama sat back, with blood all over her hands. She wiped her hands on a cloth, bent over and kissed Maria softly on the cheek. I was standing down there at Maria's feet. Mama reached down and drew the blanket over her. It cut right through the light.

'Turn the light off, Hansel,' Mama said, irritated.

As I switched off the flashlight, I saw that the barn was heaving around us as if it was alive. All the tiles had been torn off the roof and the stars were sitting on the rafters like huge white birds, like young women wearing dresses of white canvas, but they were not that, they were not women. They began to sing, a pure, high, breaking song, rushes and night water and wind moving very fast, right on top of the water, between the water and the air. There were no words to the song. You listened to it and you knew the words, but you could not say them. Maria threw off the blanket. Her body glowed with a white fire. She stood there naked. Then the blanket turned white, too. She pulled it up, a white cloak over her shoulders. The whole barn was shuddering and groaning, so loudly we could hardly hear. Mama told me to walk out then. When I did not, she took me by the hand and dragged me out. 'Get out,' she yelled – as if this was the way death came, a great hole ripped in the world and everything leaking out under pressure. But I would not go. I would not go, and then Maria saw me and came over. She took me by the hand and led me out and took me in her arms. She held me so close. She smelled of flowers! I was confused. Ja, her lips were cold on my cheek, and she said to me, 'Forget it. You have to forgive.'

But how could I, goddamn it! I never forgot and I have never forgiven. And how could she! That is what kept me awake all those years in that house in Canada as I lay on the floor and the trees thrashed in the moon and the wind – how could she forgive them when they had done that to her, the fucking bastards.

She kissed me on the cheek. Her lips were cold. She pushed me out the door. It was empty. The wind had stopped. Even the air had dribbled away. The whole earth had no smell, as it is just after a rain – that sense of things not being there, of things being clean, but absent, too, as if anything could start all over again, or happen. Anything.

In those few times I had been with Father Thomas I had come to think angels were the soul, but they were not; they were the body! To be a messenger, to go and tell things to people, you have to be made out of mud, just as people are. Angels were the body. The message God had to give us was: death and life could both see through the body; you could hold a woman and feel her life and you could hold a woman and feel her death – in the end there was only the body, and there was no death and there was no life. There was only the body, grabbing other bodies to itself and sobbing. The body brings things in to itself. It holds them. That is what it can do. That is what it is for. That is what it does. When you think about something, you just break it up into little pieces, and ja, you can hold them then, but there is not much to hold. The body was all we had. All the rest was not ours. All the rest had nothing to do with us.

The General poured four tall glasses of brandy full to the top. He passed one to each of us and to the guard and kept one to himself. It was not the sort of sleepy field of wheat you get in beer – it burned and splashed out through my body: it was alive!

'Do not worry, Madame. The men will be punished.'

'She was just a girl. If you want to go killing then kill each other, but leave the women and the children. We have already too much death.'

The General nodded and said again, 'The men will be punished.' And we went to bed.

I heard it all, and it ruined me.

21. Retribution

Morning

The bed was cold and full of sand. The sheets were as coarse as canvas next to me, as if they were woven out of nettles. My sleep was there in the room. It poured out of my mouth when I breathed and lay dead in the sheets, crumpled up and folded around me, and drained back down my throat when I breathed again, but dead when it poured back in, dead and choking. I could lie there no longer. I got up. My head was spinning. As I sat up out of my dreams and my feet touched the cold of the floor, I felt myself walking in the snow. The snow was burning through weeds in the ditch alongside a road, burning in huge flaring sheets with the cold and the wind. There was no sky. Snow whipped against my clothes and face. It was growing rapidly dark. I felt as if I was walking somewhere far away and it would take me years to get there.

As my feet touched the floor, I knew all at once that Mama was wrong. She was as wrong as she could be, as wrong as any woman ever. I had never been so sure of anything and I would never be so sure again. As I stood there and the first of the clear morning sky splashed against the window above my bed and struck over my face, and the light was clear and seemed to go on forever, I knew she thought about it, because we all thought about it – all the time we thought about it and nothing else: there was no God – we had been thrown outside the protection of any god. The only ones who could save us were our selves, but we were weak and powerless: the whole world had become God and we were no longer part of it. We were outlaws. When my Mama said she needed me to be a man, I became one for her and I did not know who I was.

The Punishment

The French called all the people of the town together into the square. There was a smell in the air of the rotten hay that had flooded in the streets in the rains. It had caught in the corners, piling up at the edges of the currents as the rain drained down through Old Town. No one had cleared it away. People used to dig it into their gardens, up there in those jumbled, stone houses, but now for the first time they did not, and it stank and steamed as it rotted in the sun.

The smell blew down the streets in the morning. There were still shadows of starlight in the gutters and doorways of Old Town. The storks were restless and jumping up on the roofs, wheeling in the air like nightmares, their wings flaring, smoke shadows over us, and behind them the sun. Giant shadow storks swept over the square, the sun whipping them around on a leash, a child's game, faster and faster, around and around and around, faster and faster and faster, and then you see where it lands, and you had better get out of the way!

Something had come such a long way to talk to us but we could not understand it. It was the smell of flowers that had bloomed under Tante Anna's hands in our basement that night that Pierre died under the leather boots of the police. It was strong and stinking in the air – some old god, walking among us, who could kill you like a partridge. And he smelled of those flowers! First he had grabbed the Moroccans, the bastards, then he had dropped them. Sweating, I quickly scanned all the faces in the square, but I could not see him. My heart was pounding. Then he came, into the hands of the French officers, with the sun like pollen on their faces and jackets and hands, and they lashed out at him to drive him away.

They made us watch those Moroccans. Everyone from the town watched, like a big crowd out of a painting, as if we had come together for a wedding or to go hunting – or to go to the circus! Big black crows circled above us then gathered in the cherry trees along Friedrichstraße and clattered and snapped at the air with their wings, like dogs bounding over each other, nipping at each other, not able to hold in their happiness.

As punishment, the French officers made the Moroccans carry a sixty-kilo pack around the village square at double speed, without food or drink, and without slowing their step for eight hours! It was a day so hot that the crows could not settle on the black slate roof of the village church above them.

The heat settled into the deep streets, and flattened out the light. It burned all around us. Slowly the people began to leave.

They drifted away, up the twisted alleys away from the square, hunched over, small in that flat light, too weak to have shadows. First they jeered and laughed, then they all just drifted away. Still the Moroccans marched around and around. As the light grew thicker in the streets there were fewer and fewer people until finally, in the heat of the afternoon, with the sun almost directly on top of us – even all the crows had left for the shade of the forest – the light grew so thick that all our shadows dissolved into it and blurred behind the men as they marched. Rudi was there for a while, and a few younger children throwing bits of gravel, and Father Thomas was there, sitting on one of his pews as the sound of the marching echoed through the hot church, the light crashing in waves, and his body throbbing. He sat with his hands over his face as the steps pounded through him. I found him there later. But even the children soon ran away laughing, scattering like cats when you come into the room with a broom. Not like dogs – dogs are smart: they hang around; they sniff things out. They do what you damn well say. Rudi looked at me from across the square and I shook my head, and he left too. Then only I was left, watching.

◎ Love

All day the sun poured into that stone square, trapped on all sides by plaster and slate. The air grew hotter all the time, until it completely burnt away. The square was an oven! The officers shifted off every hour, drinking beer in the shadows, but they made those men march hard the whole time, going nowhere but where they had stepped just the moment before. In this earth, that is what Hell is like.

Four of the men bent up and fell to the cobbles. The officers ripped off their packs and took the men to the wall of the inn, to the left of the flaking green paint of the door, on the small pile of tiles that had been blown off the roof in the shelling, that Schmidt had stacked there until he could get them back on. They shot each man through the head, once. The officers did not seem to pay them much attention, they just swore at them, and shot them, after they swore back, merde, their faces black and glistening with sweat. Every shot went through me then died down slowly, like a shot in the mountains, far away, echoing.

After eight hours the men who survived carried off the dead. The heat rustled through my pale hair like the wind through a field of ripe wheat, with poppies splashed through it, the whole field swaying.

That is where I learned about love – the love of men for each other, and how little the earth cares. I mean it does not care! Anything is OK. I no longer looked for God – I thought I had found him! I thought I had found that he was not there, that the old gods had been let loose – they had woken, and had seen us again through the fog rising off the rivers; they had shifted in their stone sleep and looked out of our eyes, and did not know what they saw, and felt trapped; felt the bone around them and felt trapped. The spell had broken which the churches had thrown over them to say they were the harmless dead. They were living – and we were their life! That was what was revealing itself all the time. I was afraid, and confused, and finally, as the square emptied of the soldiers and there was a white ring of cobbles where the dust had been scuffed off by the marching soldiers, I stood against the wall of the inn until Schmidt came out, his apron dirty and wet with beer, soaking and dark, and he wiped his hands on it, downwards, down his thighs, and told me to go home.

<hr>

☷ Stupid

When I got home, I walked straight into the dining room – maybe the French officers would have some food – and my world all came crashing down. They were not there. None of their things were there. The table had been completely cleared off, and all their things, all their maps and guns were gone. There was china on the sideboard, and wine in the wine rack, and I looked at it, and the labels were all new and crisp: 1994. I felt something slide outside of me and I was afraid. I turned around. It was as if I had died – as if I had come in the wrong door: I had pushed the door open and come in fifty years ahead of my time, yet this was my home, and suddenly I was scared.

I ran into the kitchen, but Mama was not there, only a grey coolness in the air. I pushed the back door open – it was night. As I stood there the cold slid over me and into the room. I closed the door against the night, but the cold was already in there with me.

I heard footsteps on the stair. It was a woman speaking English. 'Come on, we are late. Everyone else has already gone to church.'

I looked at her, puzzled, did I know her, and she sighed, and reached behind me to the coat rack, and passed me an overcoat. It was big and heavy. When I put it on it burnt a place into me. I did not understand.

'Come on,' she said. 'Put your coat on. We are late for church. It is cold out.'

As I looked into her brown eyes and her thin, bird-like face and saw how cold she was, I remembered everything. I remembered the angels, how God took me into the air and breathed me into the air; the stars, far and spreading out below me, the sleeping shoulder of the land. I heard the bell ringing out beneath me. Yet it was not the notes of a bell, it was nothing that was words or sound either, it was a feeling, or something you smell, that filled the air around me – peace, and pity, the unending pity that men feel for themselves in the presence of God. It was strange to me. It was wild and strange. The wind caught my wings and slowly, clumsily I moved off. The stars all around me smelled of flowers, and – then just as quickly it was gone. It was all broken. All over again it was broken. Just inches from my face was the sweaty head of Father Thomas. He was standing on the steps of the church; he grabbed my hand and dragged me in and slammed the door shut behind me and he said, his face broken, swollen in anger, 'God does not want our pity!'

22. A Dream of Gold

When Uncle Hans came home, we let him sleep in the wine room. It was a terrible place for anyone with TB. In the middle of the night when it was so dark you could not see your hand in front of your eyes I woke to the sound of coughing – a terrible, strangling sound. It went away, and I heard the sound of the sentry outside, pacing on the gravel, then it came again, a low moan. I got out of my damp sheets and slipped through the dark to Uncle Hans.

'Uncle Hans?' I asked. There was coughing again, then a hand took mine and squeezed tight.

'I have something I want to hide.' He was strangely excited. 'We are going to bury it. I need your help.'

'What is it?'

'Gold!' he whispered. He lit a match. He set it to a stub of candle, and in that candlelight we worked. The light of the candle glinted off the gold coins in his small metal chest. The gold seemed to take all the light to itself, and when I touched the coins it was as if I was touching light itself and moving it with my fingers. We used an old tin can and dug in the damp, sandy soil of the wine-room floor. At first Uncle Hans did the digging, but he started to cough again, and coughed up blood. It splattered on his fingers, black in the candlelight. The air was heavy and thick, as if all the air from Old Town had settled there, and we were digging deeper into it to bury Uncle Hans's old collection of coins, that he had from the war, for later. He never told me where they were from. The light only caught in the coins and in a grey shimmer over the floor – in a small circle around the candle. The hole was black as soot.

He said, 'They had us in a camp in the fields, surrounded by barbed wire. There was nothing to eat. They were waiting for us to die. You cannot imagine what it is like to have a million men in a field, standing in the rain. We could catch rainwater in our hats and we could grow cold. We ate grass. We took turns lying on the wet ground, while they waited for us to die. They never planned on sending us home. But we were not going to die for them. Then we started to get TB. That scared them, on the edges of those bombed-out cities, because they could get that from us.'

The candle was burning low. We set Uncle Hans's coins down in the dark of the hole, and they vanished. The last I felt was a cold, metal touch on my fingertips. It was like reaching down into someone's chest and touching their heart. We covered it in, pushing dark sand and the little chips of light on the edges of the sand over it. They fell into the darkness and vanished, too.

When we were done we scraped the last of the dust clean and laid Uncle Hans's blanket back over it. It was damned ironic, because there in the doctor's house he had to sleep down in a damp basement full of mould and bad air because the French generals were upstairs to protect us. We never thought that maybe we needed protection, that there were people who would look at Papa's membership in the party and how Mama saved Pierre and sent him across the river, and would want to kill us, would say that Mama lost the war, and Papa started it, and Mama betrayed Papa, and that we lost the war because the doctor and his wife could only fight because their marriage was falling apart, because they could not stay together; or that these people would want to take revenge on us because their sons and their brothers were dead, and they certainly had not lost the war; and if you think that is how wars are won or lost, you are wrong. War has its own life. It grows with the energy people give it, until it takes over: instead of fighting other people, you and your enemies must fight the war. That is what no-one understood about that time. In all my years in Canada, in the golden wheat fields and the glaciers under the northern lights at the end of the world, people never understood that: the war never ended; we never destroyed the war – it is inside of us, in black places, like that hole in the basement, full of gold.

◇◇

◉ Beyond Good and Evil

There are always two wars. For a while you do not know which of them you are fighting. While you fight the war as if it was the war in your head – the war in the dark, the war of storks and angels and the old gods – before you can do anything to protect yourself or to get your thoughts straight, the two wars change places: suddenly the dark is in your town, and it kills your town. There is nothing left of your town except buildings, while all that used to go on in those buildings is dead. In the fifties we thought we were so good when we said that only people mattered. We thought we could make a new world out of that. We thought there could be no more war if we did that, but we were wrong: that is what the war wanted. I do not believe in that humanism any more, but I have nothing to believe in instead. All I have is the boy I was. I thought I was growing up, but the boy I was is still there, imprisoned by the confusion of those years. He cannot get past it, because I have not let him. I made a whole new life for myself out of how much I hated men after Maria was killed by the Moroccans. 'I will be a man,' I said. I was. But I should have asked, 'Where did you get your ideas of being a man?' because they were all wrong and the boy is still there. He cannot die and he cannot come forward into this time and what am I going to do about it?

∞∞∞

⚅ Digging for Gold

I have come back to find the coins again – before I sign the house over to my sister. My brothers and I are digging in our black dress shoes and our Christmas suits. We do not find them. The electric light is burning brightly. The damp sandstone is crumbling. My brothers just crack jokes and laugh. It makes me mad.

'I saw Uncle Hans bury the gold here. He died the next day.'

'Then someone else has found it,' says Michel. 'It was Blaumann.'

'He was a good man,' I say.

'Listen,' says Michel. 'I came back from camp. We were all prisoners, all us boys who fought the war at the end. I shot down three planes with my flak gun. One came down very close to us, on the French side of the river. We went over there. There was a big Canadian hiding in a barn. We made him march back across the river, but we were just kids; we were scared stiff. He laughed at us as we marched him, and a week later we were all in camp with nothing to eat. So I said, "My papa is head chef in a big hotel in Baden Baden and I helped him all the time, so I should work in the kitchen." I worked there for a week. There was a stack of prisoner cards in the office. I found mine, signed it, and got out. When I got home I went to Schmidt's. "Maria is dead," Schmidt said. He did not say more. While I was there, Mama and Martha came. Mama begged Schmidt. "Do you have any room for two lost souls for the night?" They were all black and blue. Blaumann had beaten Mama – around the eyes. I came outside into the street. I asked, "Mama what has been happening?" She said, "Joe was so upset. He hit us. I'm scared to go back."

'I got really mad. I stormed over to the house and I yelled, "Blaumann!" He jumped me from the hallway, so I punched him in the face. He went down, like a stuck pig. I yelled, "Fuck you!" He got up again and started for me, so I yelled, "You bastard. You touch my mama or my sister again and I will kill you!"

"I will do with my wife what I fucking please!" he yelled, "You are as bad as your no-good father," and he came for me again. This time he punched me in the face. I was just sixteen. I started to bleed from my nose, so I punched him hard. He went down that time, too, so I left. As I was walking out, Schmidt came over, "What in the hell are you doing?" "He's trying to kill me!" I said. "He has beaten my mother." Then Blaumann came out and went for both of us. So then Schmidt decked him. That big pig of a man went down a third time, smashed his head on the stairs and fell in a crumpled heap. I did not care whether he was alive or dead. I left him there and walked back through town. It was deserted. The French had moved their headquarters into the castle in Rastatt, with its gold and tapestries and the painted birds on the wall. I went back to Schmidt's. "What happened?" I asked. Mama came over and cleaned up my nose and said, "I should never have married him. It is terrible to be a working woman. This is a Catholic town. I could not survive without a husband. I had to marry again. Someone had to look after the children. There were not very many men to choose from. I cannot divorce him. If I do I will be without a man a second time. After two divorces, the people will not come to me any more and to have any kind of a job I will have to move. Where can I go? What can I do about the children then?"'

23. Tradition

Rome

There are old Roman roads in the Black Forest. Every year the needles fall yellow off the trees, with polluted air from the factories that were bombed out when I was a boy and have now been rebuilt. To walk on that path is to know there is a pattern. You feel it. It all fits together somehow, across thousands of years. This is still Rome we are living in, except it has all been chopped up and broken by what we have done to it, with wars and saints chasing cats through the streets in the moonlight – the streets like milk in the white light – and the moon lapping up the water at the fountain in front of the church in the last violet light of the evening, like a red deer that has just stepped out of the forest. One minute you stand in the field and there are only trees in front of you; the next moment a deer forms out of that tangle of branches and twigs and bark and old needles and shadow – it was not there before. It all makes a pattern.

∞∞∞

The Black Forest

For a month and a half after the war there was nothing to eat at all. Franzel brought a litre of milk a day – for seven kids. She did that for many families all over town. That is all we had. After that, I went to work at Fliegehof, a big farm down in the southern Black Forest. Fliege sent me up in his orchard with his daughter, Klara. We were thirty feet in the air, shaking the branches of his pear and apple trees. The branches whipped and snapped and scratched as the hard apples and pears thundered down. The whole time, clouds grazed like sheep on the hilltops. The whole landscape looked like a fresco in the church there – a group of farmers prodding Christ with a pitchfork, with little white cherubs set into the walls, covered with bees, laughing and getting into trouble – not like the dark old church in our town. Our church squeezed down on you. You could not believe in it. At Fliegehof, I was impressed. I was young and hungry, and thought, 'It is not such a bad thing to be Catholic! Their life here is measured. Everything is in its right place. There is always food to eat!' For a while, I thought that I would become Catholic.

Klara's hair would fall loose when she shook the tree, and her breasts would shake in her dress, and leaves would catch in her hair. She looked beautiful, with her cheeks red from the fresh air. Her laughter died down after we shook the tree, and she hugged the trunk tightly while the last pears pounded down on us. It was amazing: all around her through those leaves there were those cloud sheep, on that fresco! You sensed something really old.

When we climbed down from the tree, green pears lay all over the ground. Fliege's black and pink pigs came running up, grunting, from a hole in the fence, and Klara and I had to gather the pears from among them. Pigs are pretty smart – and pretty rough. Sometimes they just pushed us over into the grass and squealed. Of course Fliege's son was killed in the war, down in Africa, using an anti-aircraft gun to shoot tanks – bombed out. That is why I was there. Klara fell in love with me. I was in love with her, too, but I did not marry her, because I also said to myself, 'It is not such a good thing to mess around with the boss's daughter. That is just trouble!' The truth is, I was young. I did not want to settle down. I wanted to be free of anyone telling me anything.

<hr>

◎ The Bee Chapel

Up in Fliegehof, we would go to church at the monastery, on a hilltop above the valley. Everyone would walk up from all the farms. A priest came in from the next village.

Fliege kept bees behind the house and made wine from the honey – he also had a still in the milk room that he used to make pear schnapps. Up there in the forest one of the white angels in the church had his finger in a pot of honey that he cradled between his legs. Little bees made out of real gold were crawling over his face. When the sun came in through the windows, the cherub was completely white – he was not stone at all any more – and the bees pulsed with honey. The monks used to make cheese up there on the mountaintop, then they taught the farmers; now the farmers make it and the monks are gone. The skills of farming have been handed down there for thousands of years. It is a tradition, and you can stand in that and be in a community.

The altar boys wore white lace dresses, the priest wore a long black dress, and they all spoke Latin, waved incense, and sang, in Latin, conjugating the verbs: *eos, is, it.* At school, I even memorized a poem by Catullus: 'Menenius' wife, Rufa the Bolognese, sucks Rufus off. She's the old bag one sees in cemeteries all the time, beside a grave, snatching the food placed on the funeral pyre....' That only got me into trouble! I did not understand a word they sang in Latin, though. Fliege, and all those other farmers up there in the forest, understood every word. I felt as if I had fallen into a deep, deep hole in time.

oooooooooooooooooooooooooooooooooooooooooooooooooooooooooooooooooooooooooooooooooooo

⊛ A Gravehouse Full of Candles and Snapshots

One time I arrived late for the mass. The choir was already singing. The people were singing back, then the organ answered them, and then the choir sang again. It was late in the year. A few yellow leaves scattered around in the graveyard. There were stone angels at each corner of the graveyard, with outstretched wings. In the back there was a stone gravehouse. The singing of the choir poured out of the church. It seemed to come from far, far away, as if it had travelled across an emptiness and was only faint when it got here and was a long, long time ago – it had got lost and wandered a long time through Time before it got to us here, and it was going to keep on going, no matter how much things changed here, and it was always going to be a long, long time ago. I realized then, for the first time, that there was a story, that it was unfolding, and that I was no longer part of that story.

I sat behind one of the gravestones. I could see way down over the Black Forest. It was very dark. Only in the clearings around those big old Black Forest barns were there yellow trees. The tall, purple and orange pear trees stood in the middle of the pastures. As I listened to the singing from the bee church, a cold fan of cloud broke against the far slope of the valley and purple sheets of snow

splashed down in straight and rigid lines then swept quickly forward. There was a rustle in the leaves of the trees; suddenly the
leaves started to stream off the branches and over the graveyard.
The air smelled of wet and snow. When the first flakes hit me, I ran
into the gravehouse for shelter. There was a shelf running around
the edge, and candles set up on it, burning, and above every candle
a picture. Most of the pictures were clipped from newspapers, but
some were cut out of schoolbooks, or were black-and-white photos
taken at a photo shop. I thought, 'Shit, people came up into the
mountains to be safe, to be cut off from things but to be safe, and
now this.' Every one of those photos was of a young man. There
were no photos of women there at all. Every one of those men was
dead. Below every photo was a clipping from the army newspaper,
saying what division the boy belonged to, where he fought and how
he died. Some of those boys were there with their Luftwaffe caps
on their heads, just sixteen, like Michel. Some of them with the
pointed grey army caps were just fifteen, just come out of the
youth camps into the war. They got on some train and got off in the
war! They died all over the place, in France or Italy, wherever.

@ The Inheritance

Maybe Mama was right, the whole problem is we try to understand
life, but there is nothing to understand, just to share. If you try to
understand, you have lost it immediately – it just breaks up farther
and farther. There are things you would like to say but you cannot
because everything suddenly floods with distance. You cannot see
that that distance is just the thing about the world, the thing the
women are talking about. You cannot understand it, though. You
cannot talk about it. It is just an immense thing between us, and
somewhere inside it and around it and through it we live. That is
what we have inherited from our mothers and fathers: all the
things they could not say. It is up to us to do something about it.
We have to reinvent the world out of scraps of propaganda. You try
to pass on a way of living to your children, so you do not have to be
a part of all that crippled silence. That is what I tried to do, there

on that orchard in Canada. I thought we could just live with the earth, could just live together, like those Catholics did up in the forest, and if there were wars we would not be a part of them. We could live on our own. We could look after ourselves.

∞∞

The End of the Storm

The snow was falling, white and silver. The wind had died. When I walked into the church there was snow on my shoes and on my shoulders. I sat in a pew at the back. Even in that small church, there were many empty pews. When the service was over, Klara walked past me and smiled. Fliege put his hand on my shoulder as he passed. I sat there while they all walked out into the snow. The light was very cool in the church, and the honeybee cherub looked cold and carved out of stone. The bees did not look joyous at all, just gaudy and cheap and even desperate. It was the same dark, cloying feeling I used to have when I was in Father Thomas's church, when during the whole war we did not see any spiders, yet as soon as the war was over there were spiders the very next day, with their webs white with dew in the grass and the rushes and the fruit trees.

When the last woman walked out, I walked out after her. The snow had stopped. We walked back to the farms in the slush. It was slippery on the way down that muddy path along the side of the hill, but that's what monks do, they build their places on the tops of hills.

∞∞

My Decision

I did not become a Catholic, either. Someone said the priest buggered the altar boys. I did not want any part of that! I decided this was not the religion for me.

∞∞

That night Fliege brought out a bottle of pear schnapps. He said, 'Hansel, do not think too much. Things are what they seem. There is Heaven and Hell; between them is this world with pretty girls and hay in the hayloft and dead boys that are only pictures in the snow. Do not think we symbolize what we do with candles: the candles are our thoughts. There is nothing else. Life is a candle you pick up, light, and set in a graveyard in the cold. It is the same with our thoughts: you see this world, you think about it, but you must not step back into this world, you must not use that thought to bring yourself back to this world, to change this world, because thoughts are like a thicket down in the Hölental – it is dark and damp down there; soon you find you are not going anywhere, and even the lovely clean water of the stream that reflected the sky, blue and white like clouds as it ran over the rills, is dark and green and black and reflects nothing; it is foreboding and you are very scared. You should be. You tell yourself it is nothing, that there is nothing there that is going to get you. You ask how anyone can believe in angels and God and Hell and Heaven in this time. You might think you have to say that to master your fear, but Hansel, we are not put in the world to master our fear. You can ride out your fear. There is only this world, Hansel. You look at it, you pass through your thoughts and you step through into Paradise, which is this world. You use your thoughts as a tool to change the world into the world. The important thing is to step through your thoughts unscathed, and when you step out on the other side your thoughts are not there. A candle is still a candle there, and an apple is still an apple and a pretty girl is still a pretty girl, and nothing more than that and nothing less. You do not make them into things, Hansel, and you do not think about them, because to think about them means you are only partway there, you are down in that thicket, in that dark black canyon and you have not yet found your way out.'

He poured me a glass of that pear schnapps. It flew through my veins like a yellow bird. I took another sip, with the small clay glass between my fingertips, and it was a bee, humming in my veins, then a whole hive of bees! I was a whole hive of bees! I could feel myself humming! I took another sip: I was the sun breaking through the clouds, a golden sun streaming in the dusty farmyard, and the chickens glowing. Even the ground was light. Fliege smiled. 'You can do it again and again,' he said. 'You can step through your thoughts again and again. Each time the world is transformed into Paradise, but only if you leave your thoughts behind, and only if you do not direct them back on the world, because that is to make the world vanish: it becomes your thoughts.' He poured us both another glassful. The pure smell of pears lifted past itself. The pure essence of pears, the thing inside a pear that makes it a pear, flooded through the room. The room fluttered. Klara came in from the dairy room, singing softly, an old song that they sing up there in the mountains.

> Nightingale, sing a pretty song
> of my proud queen,
> tell her that my sober thoughts
> and my heart are on fire
> for her sweet body and her love!

'Do not think too much, Hansel,' said Fliege. 'The priests do not tell you this. That is not why we go to church anyway. The priests have their own necessities. By *necessity* they have to live in their thoughts. They have to live in that place where thought is transformed, and look to the world without passion and to Heaven without passion, because they are the place *in between*. But you should not live there in that space, Hansel, because that is not your place. Do not turn the world into your thoughts. When you have a dream, that is real. Work for that, but *do not* think. Cheers!' And he drained his glass and I drained mine. Klara's laughter came in from the kitchen.

∞∞

⊛ A Dream of Klara

All night I dreamed of Klara. We were in a barn full of hay. All around us a mountain storm howled. There was no way we would be able to get back to the village for a week, and I kept her warm. I forced myself to wake up, and put the thought behind me. The first thing I thought about when I made that dream stop was frogs sitting in the underbrush, staring at me. The second thing I thought of was birds, rising in a black shudder out of a stubble field, the sun pale behind them. The third thing I thought of was the honey in the church, and the angel dipping his chubby little fingers into it. Fliege kept bees, too! I slipped out of my bed in the straw of the barn and went out through the sleeping chickens. It was half dark. The bees would not be flying yet. I lifted the lid from one of the hives and the warmth of the bees puffed over me, smelling of cinnamon and tears. I reached in and broke off a piece of honey. It came up covered with bees. I brushed them off, and set the lid back on the hive just as the first blue light shone between the branches of the trees on the edge of the pastures. The bees came out and danced at the entrance to the hive, then darted out and vanished into the dark. There was a rising blue glow among the trees on the ridges. I sat on a rock in the grass behind the house, chewing that wax and honey and licking it off my fingers as it dribbled. That is when Klara came out. I watched her. She was singing, just a shadow appearing and disappearing and reappearing as she moved through the air, but her voice was clear and high. I sucked the honey and watched her haul up water for the chickens and geese. They came out of the barn, warm and quiet. The workhorse whinnied softly out of the open door, and I wanted to go into Klara, to hold her and smell her hair and feel her skin tremble under her dress, but I did not. I could not do that – for in my mind I saw the straw roof of the barn burning, and felt the heat all around me. The rafters were cracking down; I was fighting through the flame to drag the workhorse out of the barn. Klara was helping me, screaming and coughing, with soot on her face, then she collapsed on the floor. The flames were roaring, loud. I could hear nothing except that roaring, like a wild and angry beast. I had to make a choice, to save Klara or the horse. It was no choice, but it was still terrible. I tried to drag them both out, but it was too hot, I had to let the horse go. It turned and panicked and ran into the fire, then it let out a horrible scream, and as the chickens ran out past me, their feathers smoking, I picked up Klara and carried her into the cool air. Away from the barn we collapsed on the grass. She was dead. I shook her by the shoulders, but when I shook her by the shoulders she was not Klara any more. She was Maria, beautiful Maria. The golden light from the burning barn splashed across the pastures in long black shadows and threads of smoke. It was not the barn. It was the sun breaking over the ridge like honey and a cock crowed.

<hr/>

◉ Farewell

In the late fall, Fliege did not need me any more and sent me home. The stars were bright then – not summer stars any more. All the sky had turned to nothing. It was not air at all. If you breathed, it felt like you were breathing the cold of the moon.

Fliege made up a big wooden box, and put a smoked ham in it, that he had up in the chimney, flour, eggs, cheese, and a pot of honey, and gave it to me. 'You can come back and work for me any time,' he said. 'You are always welcome.'

Klara drove me and that big case to the station in the cart, with the big workhorse. That morning the whole valley was covered in snow. Ahead of us there was just the white road through the trees, down to the village, for many kilometres, and behind us the footsteps of the horse and the tracks of the cart. At the station, in that small town with its red roofs, Klara asked me to stay. She said she would wait for me always. She knew I would be back. Then she kissed me on the cheek.

All the way out through the forest I thought of her and the burning place on my cheek where she had kissed me, but when the train pulled out of the trees and into the cities, pitching slowly over the broken railbed, through the ruined streets and all the piles of bricks, I started to think of Mama in that grey industrial air. It was then I realize that in all that time down in the Black Forest I had not thought of Mama at all, or Papa, or the fights they used to have. I had just thought about the trees and the farm, and Klara, and I was always too tired to dream.

When I think back on it now I realize I did have dreams, alright. They were Klara's laughter, or the bees in the church, or the fruit the fruit trees up in the pasture, or the pigs, but they were not thoughts. They were in the world. When I think back on it now I realize that Fliege was right: my life was just the place where Mama and Papa fought. All I had was the war.

24. Home

When I got back home and dragged that heavy case through the dust, I went into the house to show Mama what I had. Blaumann was there.

'What are you doing here?' Blaumann growled.

'I have come back,' I said. 'Where is Mama?'

'She is working. What do you have there?'

He dragged the case in and pried it open. He laughed when he saw all the bread and butter, wrapped in leaves, and the ham and sausage. He cut a big slice off a cheese and stuffed it into his mouth. Then he was happy. He took me into Papa's old study. He laughed and showed me all sorts of strange equipment that Mama had set him up with.

'They want a natural doctor,' he said. 'They do not believe it when your mother tells them they are healthy, so she sends them here. I give them sugar pills and test them with this equipment.' He showed me an enema machine. 'I just stick it up them, and they pay, too. Frau Schmidt even went to your mama and said it was better than anything she had ever done! You just need to know how to tell them the bullshit they want to hear.' His voice became hard and cold. 'Your papa was a doctor, too, running all over the place with the party. I remember him. Now there are two doctors in this house again!'

He went back out to get some more cheese. I said, 'I worked six months for that, we can live off that for months, it is for my brothers and sisters.'

'What a stupid thing!' he said. I do not know what would have happened if Mama had not come home. He was not the old Blaumann any more. He was not the man who knew the black market so well and could get food for us kids when no one else could. He had moved in, like a louse, sucking our blood.

When Mama came home she had a baby on her hip, a little girl! Blaumann took the baby, and Mama gave me a big hug and said, 'Hansel, you are home!'

'I have brought food!'

Mama laughed. Then she saw the piece Blaumann had cut off, and stopped. She could see the case ripped open right there in the doorway. She pursed her lips.

Blaumann said, 'What are you going to say?'

'Nothing.'

'Bullshit,' he said. 'You were going to say something. Stupid woman!' And he hit her across the face and smashed me against the wall, and walked out.

A second later he crashed back in, crushing one of the bricks of butter, passed my new little sister to me and walked out again. 'I will be at Schmidt's. You two can just be stupid together.' His voice died down as he walked away.

The baby was crying, a little girl in a pink dress. I looked down at her. Her face was red and purple. She looked really scared. I handed her to Mama. Mama wiped the tears from her eyes and took the baby. When she picked up the baby, the baby stopped crying and Mama started crying again right away, sobbing and holding the baby close. I did not know what to do. What are you supposed to do? I felt stupid. I was really mad, too. That is how I met my baby sister Margot.

I ran off after Blaumann. The tears were streaming down my cheeks.

Confrontation

I went to the Blume, to Schmidt's. Blaumann was there. I heard him shouting through the window before I went in. He was there down at the end with his friends, those men who were the first Nazis in town and who disappeared for the whole war, men missing an arm or with a black patch over an eye, the men Mama had saved at the hospital, all dressed in shabby clothes, and I realized something had changed: these men who were used to having power had no power at all any more. The whole country was in a ruin. It was people like Fliege and Mama who were all that was left of the country: Fliege in the mountains with his God and Mama with a baby and a bruised face. There, in that room, though, Blaumann and his friends still had power. But only there.

The conversation stopped when I came in. Blaumann's face was red in the light through the heavy curtain on the window. He stood up from the table.

'Get out of here before I kill you!' he shouted.

I stood my ground. 'You are a parasite,' I shouted. 'Get away from my mother.'

'She is my wife.' He sneered. He laughed and looked for laughter around the table.

Some of the men laughed.

'Leave the kid alone,' said one, an old soldier with steel-blue eyes and a burn scar running down his cheek. 'Sit down and give the kid a beer.' He stared at me. His eyes went through me like searchlights. Despite his kind words it seemed as if there was not a man in there at all; there was a machine. When he looked at me, it was as if I was not there, only the part of me that was like a machine was there and any part of me that was fire or happiness or love or hate or the trees along the path or the way I felt when a pretty girl went by, was not there. I was nothing. I looked at all the men around the table then, even Blaumann, in the yellow light of the curtain, among the stars of beer and foam. In each I saw a part that was like that. In each of them it was a different part. It was not necessarily a machine, but in all of them it was a hard, inhuman place, that stood apart, completely closed off.

I stood there, surrounded by those animals, those men who were not men. I felt my whole life there in that town then, when those sons of bitches stared at me, and I did the most important thing in my life: I left. I turned and ran. I ran all the way to Canada, all the way through the streets of the town and around Franzel's cart full of manure that she was taking herself out to the field with a wooden fork on the top to pitch it out with. I ran past the train station and over the eelskins of the river, and out into the fields, through the fruit trees and the pastures. I ran across the whole ocean and it felt like grass underfoot. I ran over the backs of whales, and out into the grass until I could run no more and could breathe no more. The whole world was heaving with my breath. I collapsed in the grass and the wind spun, the whole world spun. I closed my eyes to stop the earth, then I was spinning, but that was better: around and around, faster and faster, spinning into a smaller and smaller point of light. I did not feel as if I was lying in the grass with my eyes closed. I felt as if I was the pasture, extending outward from my arms, farther and farther. As I spun, I was the whole world turning among the stars. The sun was very bright. With my eyes closed, I was falling into the sun, faster and faster and faster, all the time over all of it and through it my breath, breathing hard, in and out, and the hammer of my heart like a drum. Then it stilled. I opened my eyes. I was in Canada. I had escaped.

<hr />

⊚ Lost Gold

My children think I tried to escape from war and politics. That is not it. I tried to escape from a trap. I tried to be a man. What did I do? I do not know. I did the same bad things to my wife. I understood her, and said I did and tried to act on that. I am afraid. This is the kind of thing you do not know what to do about, or how to talk about, until like Fliege you walk back from the war into your fields. I am standing in the garden in the snow, looking up at that big old house. That is where Blaumann will put you. That is where that fucking big picture of our Leader in the hallway will put you. Now that world is gone and Mama is dead and I am standing in the snow. My brothers and sisters are in the house. The canal is frozen. The sky is ice and heavy and has fallen low over the grey air. You can see a bright light, a bright world shining through it. But I do not want to go in just yet, damn it. There is always this pressure to go in, to be part of the group, but I want to be alone right now. It is cold. I wonder if my father thought of me like this when he was in Russia, in the snow, cutting off the feet of men with frostbite. It scares me. If you want to ask, 'What in the hell does it mean?' I will tell you. I will tell you at last.

We always said that Canada was that place we all emigrate to, to be free. I did that. Then I found out years later that in the camps in Poland, 'Canada' was a cold warehouse full of gold teeth and old shoes and wool clothes and sacks of hair and old violins, all stacked up and sorted, but no people. Now I am back and I see it was all wrong. We never found Uncle Hans's gold in the basement.

Now I stand for a long time in the cold. The stars are blue. My brothers and sisters and I are all old. We have not had a life together. When we get together like this, we are just children, fighting, but unlike children fighting about their passions and their selves, we are struggling with all the failures of our lives. It is monstrous. Whatever world was there before, the world Mama and Papa knew, pushed us out. We lived in that sense of being pushed out. We accepted that as growing up, and made a whole world for ourselves out of what was left. What was left was just broken pieces, things little kids pick up, remember, and do not understand. Out of that we made a world. And the other world became invisible.

When I go in at last, Michel is playing the piano, Bach, and Beethoven, tunes that he heard Papa play years and years ago, little broken pieces of music. As he stands there, grey-haired, bent, he is a little boy again. The whole house crackles, and I dare not move and dare not breathe.

I have come with Dorothy to sign the papers. My brothers and sisters have come from the Black Forest, from the towns of jewellers and bankers that were flattened in the war. For a year they have been fighting over this old house – without insulation, with a leaking roof, the sandstone crumbling in the basement. Some of them want to keep it. The others want to sell the house quickly, take the cash, and run, because there is nothing here worth saving. Distrust runs through the house and the family like a river. The war split us all in half. The wall went up in Berlin, but the world before the war and the world after, and those parts of ourselves bound with them, cannot speak to one another. Yet speak we must, because we were there, and we either live inside the wall and look out at our lives, and never live them, or we come out of the bunker and build a world out of old bricks and bombed-out junk. You can do what I did. I left. Some good that was. I am still here. All I wanted was to find Uncle Hans's gold. Without that, I do not care.

History follows us. We lay it on our children.

@ About the Author

Harold Rhenisch is the author of the innovative history *Out of the Interior: The Lost Country*, an *Out of Africa* about a life on the fruit plantations in the mountain valleys of British Columbia. He has also written eight books of poetry, including *Fusion*, a book of spells and invocations, and *The Blue Mouth of Morning*, a collection of Coyote and Trickster myths.

Rhenisch was raised in the German farm culture of the Okanagan, which sheltered both the innocent and the damned. Grandson of a German communist from the 1920s and two German doctors from Freiburg, he grew up into a world of story-telling, shame, and pride. With twenty-two years' experience farming fruit in the Okanagan Valley, Rhenisch now lives in the Cariboo, the high plateau between the Fraser and Thompson Rivers.